UNKNOWN WORLD

THE EMP SURVIVOR SERIES – BOOK 3

BY CHRIS PIKE

Unknown World
The EMP Survivor Series
by Chris Pike
Copyright © 2017. All Rights Reserved

Edited by Felicia A. Sullivan
Formatted by Kody Boye
Cover art by Hristo Kovatliev

To my readers: Thank you. This story would not have been possible without you and your encouragement. Y'all are the best! And to my family who has put up with all my crazy ideas and workshopping sessions, y'all are the best too.

"Effort only fully releases its reward after a person refuses to quit."
—Napoleon Hill

PROLOGUE

One hour before Chris Chandler and Amanda Hardy were in the crosshairs of a high powered Barrett M107 rifle, Kurt Durant nervously took a bite of a chocolate infused nutrition bar, swallowed hard, and said, "I couldn't get her." He held his breath and waited for his big brother Zack to hurl a string of obscenities.

Kurt had been given one order, which was to find Amanda and to bring her back to Zack.

Failure had not been part of the plan.

Sitting in a chair on the observation deck at the University of Texas Tower, Zack didn't blink, shuffle, or twitch at the revelation, only stared at his little brother who sat opposite him. He swung his Barrett M107 to the side then idly twirled the coffee he had been nursing. Zack's purposeful movements belied the fact he was seething on the inside, and the vein on the side of his forehead looked like it was about to pop at any moment.

Zack took a sip of coffee then forcefully set the mug on the table which echoed off the walls in the claustrophobic quarters causing Kurt to flinch. Using his index finger and thumb, Zack dabbed the corners of his mouth, leaned back in his chair, and clasped his hands behind his head. "Why not?" The comment was neither accusatory nor inflammatory.

Relieved beyond words, Kurt let out the breath he had been holding and ran his trembling fingers through his hair. "I don't know."

Zack's eyes narrowed onto those of his brother's, big eyes set wide apart on a baby face he had never grown out of. "You do know. I can always tell when you're lying. Your eye is twitching."

A nervous laugh escaped Kurt's mouth. "I swear we almost had her. You have to believe me. And if it hadn't been for that stupid guy I hired who said he had done work for Amanda's grandpa and knew the layout of his house, well, Amanda would be here."

"What went wrong?" Zack asked.

"Lots of things."

"Something always goes wrong. That's why you should've had a backup plan. Didn't I tell you that? I told you where she was. I told you what to do. Obviously you didn't follow directions."

"Sorry," Kurt said meekly.

"Sorry doesn't help," Zack said. After a beat he asked, "Well?"

"Well what?"

"What went wrong?"

"You're not going to let it go are you?"

"No."

"Great," Kurt said sarcastically. "Okay, on the day we decided to ride to old man Hardy's spread where Amanda was living, the weather turned bad. It was storming, lightning all around, rain came in sideways. We thought we could use it to our advantage. It was perfect cover for us. Nobody would think anyone would be out in weather like that. To top it off, Trent—the guy I hired—saw Holly and Dillon riding ahead of us."

"Who are Holly and Dillon?" Zack asked.

"People with a bounty on their heads. They were wanted dead or alive, and dead would've been much easier. We tracked them to old man Hardy's house where for some reason they stopped. They went inside so we decided to kill two birds with one stone. Kill Holly and Dillon, kidnap Amanda, and we'd be in the chips. It was perfect."

"Obviously it wasn't," Zack said.

"They were like sitting ducks in the house, practically had a spotlight on them. I don't know how it went wrong. Brent got trigger happy, but at least he plugged old man Hardy with the first round, which I'd like to remind you was on the short list of things you wanted done. After that, everything happened so fast. We both started shooting then Trent went nuts about getting the reward on Holly and Dillon."

"I don't know who those people are, or anything about the reward, and I don't care. All you had to do was get Amanda."

"Don't you even care that I stuck around town after the EMP so I could try again to get Amanda for you? Or maybe some good intel on her?" When Zack didn't acknowledge the question, Kurt tilted his head. "Well? Aren't you going to say anything? Or tell me thanks for trying?"

Zack said nothing.

"That's what I thought. I'm lucky to have made it back here alive."

Zack stared unblinking at his little brother for a long moment. Finally he spoke. "If you had taken one of my older cars as I had suggested, you wouldn't have been stuck there. EMPs don't affect cars of that vintage."

"If I had known about the EMP I wouldn't have gone there in the first place!" Kurt shouted.

"At least you had the sense to ride a bike home," Zack answered in an equally terse voice.

Kurt rubbed his left eye, trying to conceal the spasmodic twitching that afflicted him whenever he was under duress. "Trent was bound and determined to get the reward on Holly and Dillon. I tried to talk him out of it, but he wouldn't listen. Then the jackass got the bright idea to sneak in the back door and kidnap Amanda. Since he had done work at the old man's house, he knew which room was Amanda's."

"That's about the stupidest thing you could have done."

"It wasn't my idea."

"Then what happened?" Zack asked.

"He went in the back of the house, and then there was a scream and a gunshot."

"Why didn't you go in and help him?"

"We were outnumbered! It would have been suicide. We had lost the element of surprise. I found out later at the town café they didn't suspect a second person was involved. I also found out Chris Chandler was one of the guys in the house."

"Who's that?"

"A sniper, from what I learned from gossip. A real hero. Saw action in Kandahar. He helped take down the guy who had taken over the sheriff's office. He's a real big dude, let me tell you."

"And you were no match for him." Zack's tone was mocking.

"Right. You wouldn't be either," Kurt shot back. "He could whip both our asses with one hand tied behind his back."

"I doubt that, and besides I don't care about him."

Putting his hands on the table, Kurt leaned forward, dropped his voice and said, "Well, you should care, because he's Amanda's new boyfriend."

Zack rocketed off the chair. "What! A new boyfriend?" His face contorted into a mixture of rage and disbelief.

A corner of Kurt's mouth curled into a satisfied smirk. Turning the knife a little more, he said, "That's right, and they've gotten real cozy riding double on a horse." With his bravado increasing, Kurt met his brother face to face. "Your luck is about to change."

"How so?"

"Chandler is escorting Amanda to her great aunt's ranch. And you know what that means?"

"Yeah," Zack said. "They'll have to travel through the middle of Austin, past me and my trusty M107 to get there."

After Kurt left, Zack sat back down, thinking.

His plan was coming together after all, and Amanda wouldn't even know she would be leading him to what he *really* wanted.

CHAPTER 1

December, east Texas, two months after the EMP

Routine had settled in at the Double H Ranch, a five hundred acre spread in East Texas, now home to six ragged survivors, two dogs, and one scared cat. Dillon Stockdale had insisted on naming Holly Hudson's ranch the Double H Ranch, keeping to the tradition of naming parcels of land.

Earlier, Dillon had found an old bent piece of rebar, heated it, and laboriously carved the name on a board until the letters were blackened. Next on the agenda was to nail it to the posts at the entrance to the ranch. For this he would need Chandler's help.

The morning sun peeked through the low clouds, brushing the treetops, casting a golden glow over the land, awakening it. A bright red cardinal flitted from a nearby pasture to where it landed in a yaupon bush, the red berries glistening in the crisp air.

Dillon and Chandler walked in silence along the dirt road leading to the ranch entrance. Chandler carried a ladder, while Dillon held the sign.

Their footsteps were heavy and slow, and gravel crunched under their boots. A link of chain Dillon had put on each side of the sign clanged together as he walked. They passed towering pines and oaks, and tangled brambles, stopping at the gated entrance.

Chandler positioned the ladder near the posts and held it for Dillon.

The steady hammering of nails upon wood echoed across the land.

Dillon looped the last rung of the chain to a nail in the post. "I think that does it."

Dillon stepped off the ladder, and he and Chandler admired their work.

"It looks good," Chandler said, glancing up.

Dillon nodded.

The work had been bittersweet since Dillon knew this was one of the last chores Chandler had offered to help him with. This was the day Chandler and Amanda would leave. Chandler had promised to escort Amanda Hardy to her great aunt's ranch near Austin, located in Central Texas where his parents lived.

During the weeks after the big shootout in town, Dillon and Chandler had worked the land, while Holly and Amanda combined their domestic efforts to make the ranch a livable place.

Cassie and Ryan were in charge of trading goods and services, and Ryan's stint in medical school provided excellent bargaining power. He treated minor illnesses, made diagnoses, and prescribed a lot of bed rest and fluids. Hand washing was a requirement of his, and he implored his patients to be adamant about keeping their hands clean and away from their faces. Cassie was learning how to be a nurse and Ryan's assistant. They made a great team.

Electricity had been off ever since the EMP attack, forcing the survivors to lead lives much as their forefathers had led. They woke at daybreak, ate breakfast, which was leftovers from the previous night's dinner or sometimes eggs when they felt like splurging. Each had their chores, and they went about the daily business of living.

Stock had to be tended to, there was an endless supply of tasks around the ranch, and with Ryan and Chandler's help, the ranch started to shape up just in time for Chandler and Amanda to leave.

After the shootout with Cole Cassel and the resulting fallout, Chandler had been Dillon's right hand man around the ranch. He took to ranching like he had been meant to do it all his life, having a knack for repairing fences and digging latrines.

He was a big man with wide shoulders and a chiseled face, and had the hardened look of a man who had seen too much in his short years. At twenty-eight, and with a military tour under his belt, Chandler was ready to get back to a normal life—if it ever could be normal.

Days before the grid went down, Chandler had spent two nights in jail, cooling off after he had pummeled his best friend to within an inch of his life after finding him and Chandler's girlfriend in bed together. The betrayal was hard to fathom, and at first he had thought about forgiving his girlfriend, but the more he thought about it, the more he decided to cut his losses. If straying had been as easy as it had been for her after she had promised Chandler she would wait for him...well, leopards didn't change their spots. There had been earlier signs she wasn't a one-man woman, and Chandler had banged his head against the cell wall, berating himself for being such a patsy. Man, had she fooled him.

So be it.

Life went on. There were other fish in the pond, and while Chandler hadn't planned on fishing, Amanda was turning out to be a great catch.

Amanda led the horses loaded with supplies to the ranch entrance. "I just said good-bye to Holly. She said we should probably get on the road while the weather is good."

"Do you think you have everything?" Dillon asked. The words caught in his throat.

"I think so," Chandler said.

The pair was well provisioned with food to last them a week, camping equipment, and extra ammo. Amanda had insisted on taking Nipper, her dog, having made a special carrier which was attached to Cowboy's saddle.

"I guess it's time for us to go," Chandler said with pensive sadness in his voice. He put a foot in the stirrup, heaved himself up, and swung a leg over. He sat atop Cowboy, a rugged and powerful horse, cantankerous and strong-willed at times, yet when it came to the business of transportation he was the horse to depend on.

Amanda rode Indian, the smaller of the two horses, who doubled as the pack horse, carrying water, bedding, and a few tools if they were caught in a bind.

Sensing everyone's anxiety, when Chandler had said the magic phrase, "Ride 'em, Cowboy", the horse refused to budge. He whinnied nervously, stamping his front hooves. Dillon stepped closer to Cowboy and talked to him in soothing tones, stroking him along the neck and flanks.

"I'm gonna miss you," Dillon said. He took a handful of Cowboy's mane and patted his neck. "You're a good horse."

It took some coaxing to get Cowboy walking, but when he finally did, he snorted and shook his head.

"Godspeed to both of you," Dillon said.

"It's been a real pleasure." Chandler reached down to shake Dillon's hand. "I'll take good care of Cowboy, and I promise to bring him back one day."

"Holly said you can keep him. Our mare has a foal on the way, and Holly is sure Cowboy did the siring. So it won't be long until we have Cowboy number two."

"I'm not very good at good-byes," Chandler said. He glanced away and cleared his throat.

Amanda sat tall in the saddle, resting her hands on the saddle horn. "Dillon, thank you so much for everything," she said. "I don't know how to repay you."

"No need to," Dillon said. "Stay safe, and as Cassie likes to say, 'remember the Fs: faith, family, and firearms.'"

"She reminded me of that earlier. I'm going to miss her," Amanda said.

"I know. She's going to miss you too."

Amanda tapped her Glock. "As for family," she said, "I'm lacking in that department."

"You got me, Babe." Chandler winked.

Dillon cracked a smile, understanding the reference to the old song. "Watch out for each other," he said.

"We will," Chandler assured him. He tapped Cowboy in the flanks. Cowboy didn't budge.

"You need to say the magic phrase. Remember?" Dillon said.

"Right," Chandler added. "Ride 'em Cowboy!" He belted out the command using his affected Texas drawl. Taking the reins, Chandler directed Cowboy to turn right. Amanda followed his lead.

Dillon watched Chandler and Amanda until they were a speck on the horizon. He squinted and thought perhaps Chandler had turned to wave, so he returned it, unsure if he had been seen. He looked skyward, said a silent prayer for the travelers, asking the Almighty to watch over them and to keep them safe. Dillon wondered what lay ahead of them, what trials they would face, what hardships they would have to endure.

He was satisfied in their abilities, a capable man and an able woman traveling together, yet they were subject to the whims of the weather and to the vagaries of mankind they would no doubt encounter on the road.

He wondered if he would see them again, and if he did, he wondered what the world would be like then. Maybe better, maybe the same. He headed back to Holly's house where he belonged, and to where Cassie and Ryan had made a home.

There was work to be done, the day was new, and Dillon did as he always did, he barreled onwards.

CHAPTER 2

"What did you mean when you said *you got me, Babe*? Is that some sort of secret code?" Amanda asked.

"No," Chandler replied. "It's a lyric from an old song. My mom used to play Sonny and Cher music when I was a little kid."

"Cher was a singer? I thought she was only an actress. And who's Sonny?" Amanda asked.

"Long story. Cher was a singer first."

"Really? Can you sing the rest of the song?"

"I don't remember the lyrics."

"Hum it then. It's not exactly like I can plug in my music list and listen to it on my iPhone."

"I'm not much of singer."

"Doesn't matter."

"Don't laugh, okay? This is really out of my comfort zone."

"Killing people is out of my comfort zone," Amanda said ruefully, recalling the stormy night when a man burst into her grandpa's house with the intent to kill her and everyone else in the house to collect the bounty on Dillon and Holly. She realized now she had been in shock after it happened. She never gave a second thought to the Glock her grandpa had put in the nightstand in her bedroom. But when the moment came and her life depended on action, she hadn't hesitated to pull the trigger. The man fell dead in front of her and bled out on the bedroom floor. What was it Chandler had said about her? *She's got grit.* Coming from him, she took that as one of the highest compliments she had ever received.

"Try not to think about that," Chandler said. "You did what you had to do. You saved yourself and others too." Changing the subject back to lighter matters, he said, "I'll hum the tune if you don't laugh at me."

"I won't laugh. I promise," Amanda said.

Chandler cleared his throat and hummed the tune as best he could remember. He interjected a few words and hummed when he couldn't remember the lyrics.

After the brief entertainment, Chandler and Amanda rode in silence, passing the land brushed by a chilly winter wind. The dormant grass was dry and crunchy. A buzzard floated high in the sky and a mockingbird flitted across the lonely road, then landed on a bare branch of an oak tree. It sang a melodic tune and waited for another one to join in.

Miles fell behind them.

Amanda had on a pair of jeans, boots, two pairs of socks, two shirts, a jacket layered over a sweater, and a wool cap pulled down over her ears. Her long hair flowed over her shoulders, keeping the winter chill off her neck. Still, she couldn't get warm, and intermittently she shivered, both from the thought of the long trip and the cold nights sleeping in the open.

They rode like that for a while, talking at times, sometimes in silence. The winding road took them past abandoned vehicles of all makes and models. A red barn came into view and cows munched idly in the pasture. One looked up, languidly chewing cud, eyeing them. Undisturbed by the travelers, the cow lowered its head back to the ground to resume munching on the smorgasbord of winter grass.

The farm-to-market road came to a crossroads. Chandler stopped and checked the map. They took a right turn, which caused them to face the cold north wind.

They plodded on and the sun became high in the sky.

It was silent except for the rhythmic clomping of hooves upon blacktop.

"Do you think we'll ever come back here again, or see Dillon?" Amanda asked.

"I really don't know," Chandler replied.

"I was starting to get used to the place. For a while it was like home, and Cassie was becoming like a big sister to me."

"It's not too late to change your mind. We can go back."

"You can never go back." Her tone was wistful and she glanced away. "You can never go back."

"You said that as if you know what you're talking about."

Amanda didn't want to go down that emotional path or revisit memories she thought she had tucked away for good. Instead she said, "I have mixed feelings about going to Austin."

"You're telling me this *now*?" Chandler asked.

"I thought I was over all that."

"Over what?"

"Nothing," Amanda said. "I can't help the way I feel."

"Want to talk about it?"

"No."

"Are you afraid of something?"

Amanda didn't reply.

"Is it your great aunt you're afraid of? She must be like a stranger to you."

"That's not it at all."

"What then?" Chandler asked.

"Nothing," Amanda snapped. "It's not important. I guess it's just my nerves."

"Okay. If you don't want to talk about it, I won't pry. If you change your mind, you know where to find me." Chandler grinned and Amanda tossed him a forced smile.

Chandler glanced at the sky and squinted. He gauged it was past noontime by the position of the sun and the fact his stomach was growling. "You hungry?"

"Not really."

"I am, so let's stop for lunch and stretch our legs. I could use a break."

Chandler guided Cowboy to where a large oak tree fanned out over the road and part of the adjacent pasture. He went over to

Amanda, took her by the waist and helped the wisp of a girl slide off the saddle. Nipper wiggled in his carrier, which was more like a satchel, wanting to get out. Amanda scooped him up and set him on the ground. He immediately padded to a tree, sniffed it, then lifted his leg.

"Want me to gather kindling for a fire?" Amanda asked.

"No. We'll eat the food Holly packed for us," Chandler said. "I don't want to spend time making a fire."

"I could use a hot drink."

"You're cold, aren't you?"

Amanda briskly rubbed her hands together. "I'm really cold. Aren't you?"

"Not so much. Guys have more muscle mass than girls, which is why we don't get as cold."

"Remind me to work out more."

"I think you'll be getting plenty of working out soon." Chandler paused, thinking about starting a fire. "I guess we have time for a fire. Find me some twigs and leaves, and I'll get a fire going."

He dug in the saddle bags and pushed around the Stanley cook set, which consisted of two metal cylinders that fit together, one with a handle he could use to set over the fire to boil water. He placed those on the ground. He had carefully packed the rest of the contents consisting of a Quik Clot trauma pack, a LifeStraw, a Spyderco clip-it, Nalgene bottles, binoculars, a two ringed hand saw, duct tape, a survival fishing kit, and other sundry items they would need in case they ran into trouble or were delayed.

They had enough food and water to last them a week, especially if they rationed it, and for once Chandler was glad it was cold. The food would keep longer.

They couldn't afford to dawdle. Time was of the essence.

Chandler and Dillon had mapped out the trip, meticulously measuring the route using the one inch map scale to put tick marks on the map where they should stop. Chandler retrieved the map from his pocket, opened it, and silently swore. They were already behind schedule.

By car, the approximately two hundred sixty mile trip to Austin would take five hours, depending on stops, but by the horses trotting along at four miles per hour for twelve hours a day, it would take them about five and a half days. But that was by the way the crow flies. It was going to take longer. Chandler didn't want to stress the horses to the breaking point, so he decided a leisurely pace would be the best strategy. The food would last that long, and if the trip took longer than anticipated, he could always hunt.

The extra holstered Glock 17 was in the saddle bag, along with three loaded magazines. Chandler liked to be prepared.

Amanda wore her Glock and an extra magazine on a belt Dillon had given her. Chandler had made additional holes in the belt to accommodate her tiny waist, otherwise it would have slipped right off of her.

The horses grazed unattended, nibbling on grass in the fence line.

Chandler checked the area, looking for a good place to make a fire. The massive oak had dropped a copious amount of acorns and leaves, so the area under the tree was not at the top of his list. Besides, it was too shady. He liked the feel of the sun and wind on his face.

He selected a spot outside the shade of the canopy where there was a natural depression in the ground. He kicked away any loose brush and leaves that might catch fire. Satisfied the area was clear enough, he worked quickly, molding a circular firebreak, using the sandy soil as if he was making a levy.

Amanda positioned the sticks and leaves in a teepee shape, and when she finished Chandler worked his magic and got a fire going.

He constantly rehearsed his training in his mind so as not to forget vital skills, and because constant reinforcement overcame complacency. He reached into his pocket and verified the solid feel of the rectangular magnesium fire starter, recalling his training emphasizing having at least two ways to start a fire. In his other pocket, he had minimized bulk by stacking six waterproof matches together with a separate cardboard striking surface, all tightly wrapped in plastic wrap. As overkill, he carried the Victorinox Swiss Army knife model with the magnifying glass blade which worked well to start a fire on sunny days. The magnifying glass concentrated the sun's power to ignite dry leaves.

Lighters could be useful, but he didn't trust them, learning that lesson the hard way. His Zippo had leaked out after hiking over rough terrain once, and was completely empty when he needed it. Inexpensive butane lighters could work, but they would sometimes pop open when carried in hot climates.

If he was lucky enough to have his pack when he needed it, he would have extra waterproof matches, along with cotton balls treated with Vaseline. Carried in an airtight container, the cotton balls caught fire quickly and were a way to light available leaves, paper fragments, or freshly made wood shavings.

A memory of his half-civilized survival instructor came to mind: *Preparation saves time, and time saved equals saved lives.*

After the fire had sufficiently caught, Chandler added larger sticks, waited a while, then topped it with a medium sized branch.

Amanda set out the food on a makeshift table using a piece of plywood she found in the pasture. She had turned it over to make sure no scorpions or other troublesome insects had made it their winter home.

The lunch bounty included sausage sandwiches made from a feral hog Chandler had killed while he was still at the Double H ranch. The bit of dried mustard Holly had sprinkled on was a welcome surprise. The bread was thick and hearty, meant to satisfy hunger. A can of sliced peaches added the needed bit of sweetness to offset the meaty sandwich.

Sitting cross legged near the fire, Amanda held her hands up, warming them.

Nipper's nose twitched at the aroma filling the air, and he waited with anticipation for a handout. He padded to Amanda and sat on his haunches. She reached out and absentmindedly scratched him behind his ears.

"I forgot the bottled water," Chandler said as he stoked the fire. Can you check for the bottles in the saddle bag? And grab a pack of tea or hot chocolate mix."

"Which do you want?"

"It doesn't matter," Chandler said.

Amanda went to the saddle bags and dug around. Peeking in, she saw a bottle of Lawry's. "What did you pack Lawry's for?"

"I couldn't resist. Everything tastes better with Lawry's. Salty food becomes a luxury during times like these."

"Where'd you get it from?"

"The grocery store in town that had been looted. The shelves were picked clean, but most of the spices were still there."

Amanda laughed. "Never figured you for much of a cook."

"There's a lot you don't know about me," he said as she headed back to the makeshift table.

She handed both a bottle of water and a package of hot chocolate mix to Chandler. He poured the water into one of the Stanley containers, put the lid on it, opened up the handles, and placed it on the fire.

"Why did you put a lid on the container?" Amanda asked.

"Water boils faster that way. Don't you know that?"

"Yeah, sorta." She looked away. "I know it now."

For the rest of the meal, they ate in silence with only the sounds of the country keeping them company. A brush of wind came by, blowing around strands of Amanda's auburn tresses. She tucked them behind her ear and ran her fingers through her hair, untangling it. Nipper sat patiently on his haunches, waiting for a piece of sausage. Amanda finished half her sandwich and picked at the other half, which didn't go unnoticed by Chandler.

"Are you going to eat the other half?" he asked.

"No, this is about all I can eat."

"You should eat when you have the chance because you never know how long it will be until the next meal."

Amanda took another bite and washed it down with a gulp of water. "I'll give the rest to Nipper."

"Give him the meat. I'll eat the bread. I had to cinch my belt buckle another notch yesterday."

When lunch was over, Chandler kicked dirt over the hot coals. Amanda returned the piece of plywood to where she had found it. They cleaned the area, leaving no trace they had been there.

Chandler helped Amanda onto her horse, then he mounted his. Nipper was tucked away in his carrier and the travelers headed west along the blacktop road, each lost in their own thoughts and eager to reach their destination.

CHAPTER 3

Another day wore on. Low clouds rolled in, hiding the winter sun and the warmth it brought. The cold gripped the travelers, uncaring about the misery it unleashed.

Amanda shivered as the cold seeped through her clothes. Her ears hurt, and she tugged down on the wool cap and bunched her hair around her ears. Her fingers were numb and she flexed them to bring back circulation.

Being cold was getting weary.

"Ride with me," Chandler said.

"Won't that be too much weight for Cowboy?"

"He'll be able to handle it."

"What about my horse?"

"I've got extra rope. He'll follow just fine."

Riding double on Cowboy, Amanda held herself tight against Chandler. A break in the clouds brought relief and she turned her face to soak up the remaining warm rays.

Chandler had become worried about Amanda. Normally chatty,

she hadn't spoken in the last hour.

"Are you okay?" he asked.

"I'm cold, that's all. I'll be okay." Her teeth chattered and her speech was slow and deliberate.

Chandler was alarmed at the thought Amanda might become hypothermic. He had felt her spasmodic shivers for the last hour and what he needed to do was to find shelter for the night. They were on a long stretch of road in a sparsely populated area and he hadn't seen anywhere he could stop. He kept a lookout for any type of structure, perhaps an abandoned barn or house. Even an old sharecropper's house would be sufficient. He was wary of asking strangers for help, and while they might seem amiable at first, desperate people would act and say most anything for the chance to abscond with their supplies.

The next town was a half a day's ride from where they were, so stopping at an inn, even if it had been deserted would have to wait.

Another quiet and cold hour later, before dusk darkened the land, Chandler spied an old derelict house set back about a hundred yards from the road. It appeared to be a tangled growth of vines and saplings until Chandler noticed the rectangular pattern. He turned Cowboy and headed in the direction of the house.

Amanda didn't even notice when Cowboy stepped off the blacktop and onto a dirt road.

Cowboy sensed the traveling for the day was coming to an end and he picked up the pace without instruction. Chandler drew back on the reins to keep him from an all-out run.

The rundown house had definitely seen better days. From a distance, it was obvious the front porch roof was sagging. A vine, now dormant in the winter, snaked up one of columns and onto the roof. An overgrown ligustrum was more like a tree instead of a bush.

The rusted, corrugated roof disappeared into the canopy of branches and vines that scraped the roof, and when the wind blew it sounded like fingernails on a chalkboard.

Behind the house was a shed of sorts, more like an open air barn that had become a dumping ground for farm relics from the late 1800s. A stall for livestock would be a suitable place for the horses to spend the night sheltered from the wind.

Chandler guided the horses to a large gap in the chain link fence. Stopping at the porch, he slid off Cowboy, careful not to knock

Amanda off. She appeared to be sleeping sitting up.

He let Nipper out of the carrier and the dog apprehensively took in the new surroundings. He went to the porch steps, sniffed, and left his mark.

Chandler quietly retrieved a bedroll, looped it over his shoulder, then reached up to Amanda. He slid her off the saddle, scooped her in his arms, and carried her to the house. Nipper followed behind.

Walking up the rickety porch steps, he peeked into the house through one of the grimy windows. There was no movement or any sign of recent human habitation.

The front door was ajar so he pushed it open. A musty smell greeted him as he entered the cold and dark house. Nipper went to a pile of animal scat and sniffed it. No doubt a raccoon had made this his home at one time. An old sofa sat against a wall. On the opposite side was a chest of drawers.

Using one hand, Chandler rolled out the sleeping bag onto the sofa.

He carefully set Amanda on the sofa, stretched her out, and covered her with the sleeping bag. Nipper, being the protective dog he was, jumped up on the sofa to stay with Amanda.

Working fast while there was still daylight, Chandler went outside, found a couple of boards, and tied them in place to fill the gap in the fence. He unsaddled the horses and removed the bridles letting the horses graze while he worked. He retrieved the Stanley cook set, food, water bottles, and a handful of dog food. He brushed the horses once and checked each hoof for any sign of lameness.

Walking back inside, he set the items on a table.

Amanda was sleeping soundly.

Chandler unclipped his ASP Scribe flashlight from his front shirt pocket. A high-powered flashlight for its diminutive size, which was no more than the length and width of a pen, the beam had the ability to blind. He had been surprised that it worked after the EMP, but having it stored in a metal gun safe probably protected its electronics. It had been a good luck gift Dillon had given him for the trip to Austin. He clicked it on and gave the interior a onceover. The ceiling was peppered with mud dauber nests, a problem for sure in the summer, but not now.

A wood-burning stove sitting in the middle of the room appeared to be workable and similar to the one at Amanda's grandfather's house. Chandler brushed off a decade's worth of dirt and debris and opened the door, gauging if the thing was safe to use. He also checked for any unwanted guests. He cleaned out an old rat's nest and shined the flashlight in looking for any beady eyed reflections.

So far so good.

Remembering the pile of firewood stacked against the house, he retrieved a few logs, shaking them out before entering the house to make sure there were no black widow spiders or scorpions hiding in the crevices.

He cleaned out the old ashes from a previous use, tore out pages of magazines someone had set near the stove and removed a newspaper still in a plastic wrapper.

Taking two pieces of firewood, he placed them on the side, positioning them so there was a space in between them to create a heat chamber. Next he put the rolled up newspaper and loose magazine pages in the space, followed by kindling and larger logs. He lit the newspaper with a match, and soon the kindling caught. He closed the door, leaving it open a crack for ventilation, and stepped back.

Chandler shrugged out of his coat and draped it over the sofa where Amanda slept. She shifted, yawned, muttered something, then it was quiet again. Nipper lay curled in a ball at her feet.

Five minutes later, he checked the fire. It was roaring, giving off an incredible amount of heat.

Chandler placed the dog food on the floor then went about the mundane business of eating by himself. He silently ate the rations, chewing deliberately. He wasn't hungry and ate more for sustenance than pleasure. He gave the last bite to Nipper, who had been waiting patiently for a handout. It was the third venison sandwich Chandler had eaten since they left the safety of Holly's ranch. The simple meal satiated his hunger, so at least that was positive.

He went to the kitchen and checked the cupboard, not expecting to find anything useful. To his astonishment, he found a kerosene lantern which still had fuel in it. He struck a match to light it.

The kitchen was nothing to write home about. Whatever appliances had been there had been removed or stolen, a broken dish had been left on the counter, and the rusted sink had a layer of grime obscuring what at one time had been white porcelain. A chewed up box of rat poison was on the floor, along with a box of what appeared to be cereal that had been ripped into and gnawed on.

There was nothing of use in the kitchen so Chandler stepped back into the room where Amanda slept.

The wood-burning stove had warmed up the room to the point he had to remove his outer shirt, leaving him with a t-shirt.

Boredom had become an ever present reality in the post-EMP world. No more computer searches, video games, or even television. Chandler's mind was ever active, and he did not relish a boring night after such an exhausting day. He spotted a long, interesting wooden box on top of a chest of drawers.

He opened the box to find an old style sharpening stone. Fourteen inches of micro porous stone that felt smooth to the touch, yet the pores were sufficient to remove a precise amount of steel to sharpen a razor or a knife. Long stones like these were a thing of the past since the invention of modern diamond sharpening stones.

Chandler's hand went to the sheath of his SOG Bowie. He touched the outer pouch containing a three inch diamond stone that he used out in the field. He opened the snap and pulled it to reveal a blade nearly ten inches in length. It had a good edge, but he wanted to turn it into a great edge.

He placed the stone on the table and went to work.

He positioned the blade on the nearest end of the long stone and used both hands to keep the angle steady as he pushed the blade to the end of the stone. When at the end, he pulled the blade back toward his body in a long, circular motion, continuing the process until he deemed the side was polished enough. He then flipped the blade to repeat the process on the other side.

Two hours passed surprisingly quickly. Chandler was almost finished, feeling the smoothness of the new edge.

Chandler's Uncle H.V. had taught him how to sharpen knives, including one last trick to see if the process was finished. He put the knife edge facing away on a paper towel and pulled it back to him. If the edge passed over the paper towel without grabbing it, then the edge was perfectly smooth.

He flipped the knife to test the opposing edge.

His knife-sharpening skills passed the test. The edge was perfect. If there had been any resistance he would have resumed polishing.

With a satisfied grin he slid the knife back into its synthetic sheath. Anyone that faced this knife now would be in for quite a surprise.

Amanda woke groggily and rubbed the sleep out of her eyes. "Where are we?" she asked. "And how did we get here?"

"You fell asleep while we were riding. I thought it would be a good idea to stop and get you warmed up. How do you feel?" Chandler asked.

"Okay, I guess. I'm not cold anymore. I didn't realize how cold I was."

"You were worrying me," Chandler said. "You were becoming hypothermic."

Amanda sat up and pushed the sleeping bag off of her. "I feel much better. What time is it?"

"I don't know. Check your pocket watch, the one your grandpa gave you."

"I forgot I had it." Taking it out, Amanda flipped it open. "Almost eight." She closed it and placed the watch back into her pocket. "Is there anything to eat?"

"Come sit here at the table and I'll make you dinner."

"What's that on the stove? You cooking something? Soup by any chance?" She rubbed her hands together briskly at the thought of hot soup.

"Tomato soup and grilled cheese is unfortunately not on the menu tonight."

Amanda's shoulders dropped.

"But we do have hot tea."

Chandler poured Amanda a cup of hot tea into one of the Stanley cookware containers. Steam from the hot tea wafted upwards, and Amanda wrapped her hands around the cup, warming them. Chandler offered a venison sandwich and bottled water to her. She greedily ate the entire sandwich, along with a helping of canned peaches. She finished the hot tea then gulped down the entire bottle of water.

"I didn't realize how hungry and thirsty I was."

"You've been shivering and burning a lot of calories. It's easy to get dehydrated in cold weather without knowing it."

"How much further to Austin?"

"Several more days. I can only push the horses so much considering they're packing extra weight. Forty miles a day is the limit." Chandler leaned back in his chair and studied Amanda. "I've been thinking about something you said."

"What was that?"

"About how you can never go back. What did you mean by that?"

CHAPTER 4

Good question, Amanda thought.

One she didn't want to answer. Rising from the chair, she went to the window, staring out into the cold black void. The wind whipped the shutters and whistled up through the eaves of the house. Nipper had returned to the sofa and curled into a snug ball atop the sleeping bag. Even though it was warm in the room and Amanda had removed her coat, a sudden chill captured her and she shivered. Her back was to Chandler.

"I was in high school when I met him."

"Him? Who are you talking about? An old boyfriend?"

"I was at a gas station pumping gas and having a difficult time with the nozzle. For some reason, I couldn't get the gas to pump. This guy came over and asked if he could help me. I told him he could. He laid on the charm, complimenting me, asking me what college I was going to." Amanda shook her head at the memory. "I can't believe how gullible I was. It disgusts me now, but at the time I was so flattered he thought I was older. When you're a seventeen year old girl, all you want to do is to look older. I told him I was still

27

in high school and when he asked which one he said he had gone there too. We even had some of the same teachers so I knew he was being straight with me. I was so stupid. I knew he was older, but I didn't realize how much older."

"How much older?" Chandler asked.

Amanda swiveled around and met Chandler's eyes. "Ten years."

"Quite an age difference between seventeen and twenty-seven. That's basically my age now. I can't believe your parents would let you date someone so much older than you."

"They didn't. I understand now there's a big difference between seventeen and what I am now," Amanda said. "At the time I didn't because teenagers think they know it all." She stepped away from the window, walked over to Chandler, and sat down next to him.

"Amanda, we all went through that phase, including me."

"I think I've aged ten years in the last few months." Amanda's voice was repentant and her gaze dropped to the floor. She picked at a ragged hole in her sweater, pulling a thread.

With a gentle hand, Chandler lifted her chin. "You don't look ten years older, in fact, when I met you I thought you were still in high school."

"My grandpa said someday I'll appreciate not looking my age."

"Your grandpa was a smart man. I wish I could have known him."

"He was a good judge of character and I could tell he immediately liked you."

"I immediately liked *you*," Chandler said.

Amanda smiled. "And me *you*."

Nipper was curled into a tight ball on top of the sleeping bag. His eyes were open and he was listening to the conversation. Not the words, which were meaningless, but rather Amanda's and Chandler's tone and body posture. Nipper had studied his mistress long enough to understand she was experiencing physical and mental stress, which manifested in her sluggish movements and furrowed brow. Nipper was still getting to know the man, seeing he was new to the equation, adding a mixture of confidence and tenderness. He had never raised his voice or hand in anger, yet the maleness of his persona could not be dismissed. He was a man that commanded respect.

Nipper uncurled from his sleeping position, rose, and stretched in the way dogs do. He jumped off the sofa and padded over to

Amanda. Looking at her, he waited until she patted her thighs, encouraging him to jump in her lap. At the first pat, Nipper jumped into her lap with the ease of a cat. Amanda stroked him along the ruff on his back, then behind his ears, finishing with a scratch between his eyes.

"Has he eaten?" Amanda asked.

"Yes. I fed him while you were sleeping."

"Thanks."

"Tell me the rest of the story," Chandler said.

Amanda let out a big breath as she petted Nipper. The connection seemed to calm her. "I had to sneak around because I knew my parents wouldn't approve of the age difference. I had been a straight A student, involved in the Honor Society, drama club, this club, that club. You name it, I was in it. I was the poster girl for being involved."

"You talk about being a straight A student in past tense. What do you mean by that?"

"When I first started seeing Zack, my grades were perfect. I was on cloud nine. I tingled at the thought of him. He was so…what should I say…" she paused, searching for the right word, "…so forbidden. A bad boy. He was the apple in the forbidden garden. Not to be touched or tasted or experienced in any way." Amanda lifted her gaze and made direct eye contact with Chandler. "Am I embarrassing you?"

"No."

"I couldn't study, couldn't eat. My grades dropped."

"Didn't your parents notice?"

"They did," Amanda confirmed, "but I told them my classes were hard and that I was stressed out."

"Hmm."

"I thought I was in love with him. After my parents went to bed, I would sneak out of the house through my bedroom window. We had a two-story house with a weirdly shaped roof that sloped across the front part of the house. I would leave the bedroom light on so Zack would know I was in my room. He'd park on the corner and when it got dark, he'd whistle—sorta like an owl hooting—to let me know he was waiting for me. All I had to do was to walk down the ramp, slide off the roof, and Zack would whisk me away in his truck. We'd go to his apartment. Drink, listen to music, and…" Amanda paused, "… and other things." She dropped her eyes, unable to look at Chandler. "I'm not proud of that."

"It doesn't matter to me."

Amanda nodded.

"I take it he wasn't a dinner and a movie kind of guy."

"We never went out. I was too afraid someone from school would see me. I never even told my best friend. Besides, Zack was afraid of being busted. Remember I was only seventeen. His friends knew about us because he liked to brag to them. They would be at his apartment sometimes, crashing on the sofa. They never seemed to have jobs, just sat around and watched TV and drank. I couldn't understand why Zack hung around those guys."

"Did he have a job?"

"Yes. He worked at an auto repair shop. He could fix just about anything with wheels on it. He was quite good, and talked about opening up his own repair shop."

"Did he?"

"I don't know. Something changed in him, or maybe he had been like that all along, which is what I suspect now. At the time, I was too blind to notice. It was like I couldn't do anything right. He was always criticizing me. I was stupid and thought that's what the guy in a relationship did. Whenever I started talking about going to college, he'd tell me college was a waste of money and only for nerds. I challenged him on that and he hit me. Left a big bruise under my eye."

"What did your parents do?"

"I lied and told them one of the rafters on the stage ceiling fell and hit me when I was working on a play."

"They believed you?" Chandler asked incredulously.

"Why not? I had never lied to them before."

"Your parents found out eventually, right?"

"They did."

"How?"

"One night when the furnace stopped working, my mom came up to my room to give me another blanket. I wasn't in my room, and the window was open a crack, and that's when they found out I had been sneaking out of the house. They waited up for me and confronted me about what I was doing. Now that I look back on it, I was relieved they had found out and made me stop seeing him.

They gave me an ultimatum that I could break up with Zack or else they wouldn't pay for college. Quite frankly, it was an easy decision. I realized I didn't love Zack and that he was only a teenage crush I had outgrown. When I told Zack it was over, he went ballistic, saying all sorts of bad things about my parents, about how he'd make them pay." Amanda dropped her chin and glanced away.

Chandler picked up on her change in demeanor. "What's wrong?"

"I miss my parents. I feel guilty because there were times I wanted them dead," Amanda said.

"All teens think that at one time or another about their parents," Chandler said.

"Yeah, but if it hadn't been for Zack, they'd still be alive."

CHAPTER 5

Zack Durant stood on the observation deck at the University of Texas Tower, cursing and waiting for his shift to end. Cold wind whipped around him. He peered out over the campus while he sighted unsuspecting travelers through the crosshairs of his 50 caliber Barrett M107 rifle.

He pulled the collar of his winter coat up around his neck and stamped his feet to get his circulation going. He paced the narrow corridor of the observation deck, which afforded a 360 degree view of the city.

On a clear day, visibility was fifteen miles.

To the east was I-35, and beyond that was the poor side of town, the side of town with knife fights and killings over a few dollars. South had a good view of the capital and downtown area. West was suburbia and Dellionaires, and their mansions and fast cars, nestled in and among the hills. To the north was cookie cutter suburbia.

Situated in the middle of the famous forty acres, the three hundred foot high tower boasted twenty-nine stories and hailed as a distinguishing landmark in Austin. It was the scene of a mass murder in the 1960s where a deranged sniper picked off unsuspecting students and anyone unlucky enough to be in the crosshairs. The limestone walls of the observation deck still bore the scars of bullet holes.

The Tower, originally built to house the library of the University of Texas, had a closed-stack catalog system requiring students to request a book and wait for up to an hour for it to be retrieved. As the university grew, it soon became obvious a more modern library was needed for the closed-stack system. The way of the calling system for books went the way of the horse and buggy. The building now contained administrative offices and reading rooms for students.

Zack, always an opportunist, had seen the EMP attack and the resulting effects as a way to propel his life's ambition, which was to control as much as he could, anyway he could.

In the years since his break-up with Amanda, he had opened up three car repair shops, hired the best mechanics, charged ridiculous prices, but if there was one thing Zack was good at, it was opportunity.

Four years prior, he set up the first shop on a lot in east Austin dotted with scrub brush, surrounded by unsavory shops and even more unsavory houses, rented by equally unsavory characters. Gunshots and fights were common, but as word got around Zack delivered on what he promised, business boomed. His ads were all over TV, and at first he was the laughingstock of the city until it became clear he was building a car repair empire and becoming a reputable businessman.

Man, had he fooled everyone.

Inside, he was still the kid from the wrong side of the tracks that couldn't get the girl he wanted. And though he could have had any woman he wanted—and many did want him—the only one he had pined for had left town.

If only Amanda could see him now and how successful he had become, she would have seen how foolish she had been. They could have had an innately satisfying relationship if it hadn't been for her old-fashioned parents and their insistence she call it off with him or they wouldn't fund her college education. It was him or college, and the books won out. Zack couldn't let that happen.

Payback for her parents was a bitch. A wicked smile spread across his sharp features as he recalled sneaking over to their house and cutting the brake line on her dad's car just in time for them to go out for an anniversary dinner. Zack had even followed them home from the restaurant so he could see his handiwork in action. He watched with sick curiosity when the car went out of control and left the highway, plowing down the hillside cedars. The icing on the cake happened when it flipped over and caught fire. The local news reports the next morning confirmed the two had died.

Zack even went to the funeral to offer his condolences, but that damned great aunt of Amanda's told him to get lost. He smirked. Payback for her had been a bitch too.

Zack couldn't understand why Amanda revered a college degree. Plenty of PhD types had walked into his shop not even knowing even where to find the battery in their car.

For such book-smart people, they were as dumb as posts and gullible when it came to the reasons for repairs. Zack had figured out the PhD types didn't want to let on how inept they were when it came to car mechanics, so he talked in repair-speak so fast, peppering it with all sorts of confusing reasons the car needed work, the PhD types agreed to the repairs so as not to appear ignorant.

When it came time to pony up the money, Zack made sure to charge Clydesdale size hourly rates.

Regardless of how much he thought about business, his mind kept circling back to Amanda. The more Zack thought about Amanda, the angrier he became, and this boring shift made things worse.

He couldn't quell his thoughts.

Amanda had skipped town to whereabouts unknown until a newspaper published an article about urban sprawl encroaching upon her great aunt's ranch. The last paragraph contained vital information about a brother living in East Texas. A quick check by a private detective confirmed Amanda was staying at her grandfather's ranch.

He had sent Kurt to East Texas to do his dirty work, then the EMP struck, and without communication he had no idea what had happened to his brother *or* to Amanda.

His plan appeared to be falling apart.

UNKNOWN WORLD

Zack thought about using his 1970 cherry red Chevy Malibu he had bought years ago for pennies on the dollar. But driving that to East Texas would for sure put a bulls-eye on his forehead. He had rebuilt the engine, painted it, replaced the tires and rims, and drove it like he was a big man on campus which, as of now, he was. And if he left Austin, no telling what would happen to his new empire.

Without a working financial system, cash had become useless, and the goods and services customers offered to trade for his service were laughable. He found it humorous regarding one desperate man who offered his teenage daughter. Zack was more disgusted by it than tempted, and had sent the man scurrying for cover when he pointed a rifle at him. The said rifle was the Barrett M107 which he was now the proud owner of. When he pressed the guy he bought it from where he got it, he said he had taken it from a deserted National Guard station. That rifle was worth the work he had to put into the guy's car, and in the weeks following the EMP, Zack only took guns and ammo as payment for services. He realized the better armed he was, the better chance he'd have at building another empire.

He traded precision repairs for precision shots—both of which he excelled at.

Zack walked the west facing side of the observation desk and smirked at the throng of sheeple strolling mindlessly along the empty streets, unaware of their surroundings, making small talk and laughing.

Just for fun, Zack sighted an old man in the crosshairs, tracking him as he shuffled along the sidewalk, dragging his belongings behind him. When the man came too close to the boundary Zack had made around the university, he blasted a round near the old man. Seeing the man hop and do a little jig made the mundane shift worthwhile.

Zack was a wolf among sheep, and he wielded sharp shears in the way of the Barrett M107, and his unrestrained use of it.

CHAPTER 6

"What do you mean if it hadn't been for Zack your parents would still be alive?"

Amanda set Nipper down on the floor and went to the doorway entering the kitchen. Disregarding what Chandler had said, she asked, "Is there anything in there to eat?" She didn't expect to find anything—it was more out of habit and gave her some semblance of normalcy.

"Nope. Already checked."

"I'm still hungry."

"That's a good sign. How about some of the caramelized pecans that you and Holly made?"

"That would be great. We made them with white sugar instead of brown sugar. They weren't quite as good, but they'll satisfy anyone's sweet tooth."

Chandler dug around in the bag containing the carefully rationed food. "Come sit back down."

They had enough bread and jerky to last them several more days. The canned peaches were quickly being consumed, but they still had a good supply of pecans thanks to the crop that had matured right before they left. Sitting around the fireplace at night at Holly's place cracking shells reminded Chandler of his own home and the good times they had doing the same thing.

"You haven't answered my question," Chandler said.

"I was hoping you'd forget."

"I haven't."

With a rueful expression, Amanda said, "They died in a car crash about a month after I broke up with Zack. I can remember it like it was yesterday. I had finally won back the trust of my parents and they decided it was okay for me to stay home by myself. My parents forgave me without any strings attached. They said I had learned my lesson."

"That's the way most people learn."

"I know. It was their twenty-fifth wedding anniversary and my mom and dad wanted to go eat at a fancy restaurant downtown. It was a weeknight, and since I had a test the next day, I couldn't go with them. They were glad I was buckling down to bring up my grades so they didn't press me to join them. Sometimes I wish I had been in the car with them." Amanda looked away, swallowing a lump in her throat.

Chandler gently pinched his thumb and index finger on her chin, turning her head so she had to face him. "I'm glad you weren't."

Amanda nodded. "I had stayed up late studying and the time got away from me. Next thing I knew it was near midnight when I realized they weren't home. I called my mom's cell phone, but she didn't answer, and neither did my dad. I was getting worried because they said they'd be back by ten. My dad liked to watch the ten o'clock news. He especially liked to watch the latest weather forecast even though he always complained about how wrong the forecast was."

Amanda dropped her chin to her chest and the tears came easily.

Chandler wrapped his arms around her. "It's okay. I'm here."

"I'm..." she hiccupped, "...okay."

Chandler patted her on her back and smoothed down her hair.

Amanda wriggled free from Chandler, sniffled, and swiped under both eyes. "Around one a.m. there was a knock at the door and there were two policemen standing there. They asked if anyone else was home, maybe an older sister or brother. I told them I didn't have any brothers or sisters. I knew something had to be wrong and they didn't want to tell me at first, but finally did. It was the worst night of my life."

"I'm sorry to ask, but how'd they die?"

"A car crash. A single vehicle accident. They were on FM 2222, it's that winding steep road like the roads you see on car commercials."

"I know it well," Chandler said. "I've driven it many times. It's a dangerous stretch of road on the cliffs above the Colorado River. What happened? Were your parents drunk?"

"The toxicology tests came back negative, no alcohol or drugs. The police said something must have happened to make my dad lose control of the car. It veered off the road and rolled over several times. Last time I drove that road, you could still see where the cedars were mowed down."

"Maybe he swerved to miss a deer?"

"There were no skid marks."

"I still don't understand. What does it have to do with Zack?"

"The insurance investigation uncovered the fact the brake line had been cut." After a beat Amanda asked, "And *who* would know how to do that?"

"Zack."

"Exactly what I've been thinking," Amanda said.

"He got away with murder?" Chandler asked.

"I think so."

"Did the police do anything? Question him?"

"They did, but he had a rock solid alibi."

"Let me guess," Chandler said, "he was with a friend."

Amanda paced the length of the table. "Yeah. One of the guys that used to hang out at his apartment."

"Now I understand why you're reluctant to go back to Austin."

"That and the fact I'm not looking forward to staying with my great aunt. Her ranch isn't that far from west Austin. Urban sprawl was encroaching close to her ranch, and by now it might be a strip mall for all I know."

"When was the last time you saw her?" Chandler asked.

"My parents' funeral. She's like a stranger to me, and I don't even know if she wants me."

"Then why go?"

"My grandpa said to."

Chandler thought about that last statement and what he knew about Amanda going to live with her grandpa after her parents died. She had been seventeen, a difficult age in anyone's life being on the cusp of adulthood, yet not old enough to be on their own. Jack Hardy would have been the only family she had.

"Is there a bathroom in here?" Amanda asked.

"Yes, but I wouldn't use it."

"I can wait until the morning, but I still need to wash up before I go to bed. I smell like a horse."

"It's down the hallway," Chandler said. "Take the lantern with you in case there are any visitors."

Amanda gave him a questioning look.

"Creepy crawlers."

Digging in her backpack, she found a small bar of soap wrapped in wax paper. She excused herself to what was left of the bathroom.

Debris littered the rusted tub and contained what appeared to be a mummified rat. Fur remnants lined a pointy jaw.

Amanda set the lantern on the back of the toilet and grimaced at the toilet contents, now black and crusty. Afraid to touch the lid, she balanced on one leg and used her other foot to close the lid. When it hit the seat, it made a loud thud. She quickly disrobed and set her clothes on the sink. Taking a rag she found in the bathroom cabinet, she spread it on the chipped tile to keep her bare feet off the grimy floor. She carefully unwrapped the soap from the wax paper wrapper, dribbled a small amount of water on her body, under her arms, and in other places the sun didn't shine on, rubbed soap over her body, then splashed the remaining water over her back and chest, letting the water run down her legs and feet.

A chill captured her and she shivered from head to toe. Her hair was a greasy mess, but thankfully long enough to pull back in a ponytail. A good shampoo would have to wait.

* * *

During the night, Chandler lay awake listening to the blustery wind whipping the house, and to the crackling of smoldering embers shifting in the stove. He tossed and turned until finally he fell asleep. Sometime in the night he awakened to cold air filling the room.

Shrugging out of the sleeping bag, he added another log to the wood-burning stove to ward off the ever-present winter chill.

He checked on Amanda sleeping snugly on the sofa with Nipper curled next to her, and for a moment he thought about the difference between her and his old girlfriend Crystal. Physically, they couldn't be more different. Crystal was statuesque and the stuff of dreams, while Amanda was petite, but as she said, "Dynamite comes in small packages." From the first time he saw her in the barn at her grandfather's place, he sensed an immediate and reciprocal attraction, but after Crystal's betrayal, it was hard for him to let his guard down. Nobody would do that to him again. Ever.

He pulled the sleeping bag up to his chin and after a bit, his eyelids got heavy. He drifted in and out of restless sleep. Regardless how hard he tried to forget Crystal, his thoughts kept drifting to her and the betrayal he couldn't forget.

* * *

Chandler woke in the morning with fuzzy thoughts about a dream he had about Crystal, and for some reason his anger toward her wasn't as raw as it had been. For a long time, he had buried it deep down where the hurt wasn't visible. He had thought his life would have been with Crystal, and at first he wished he had never walked in on her and his best friend. In hindsight, it was the best thing that could have happened, otherwise, he would have never met Amanda.

CHAPTER 7

When morning came, the wood-burning stove only had coals left in it, and since Chandler wasn't willing to waste time to boil water for hot tea, he and Amanda ate a cold and meager breakfast consisting of wild hog jerky, bread, and a granola bar, washed down with bottled water. Plastic water bottles had been refilled using water from the well at Holly Hudson's place. It had a different taste than city water. The best Chandler could describe it was having an earthy aftertaste. He was careful not to shake it, nor stir it, although a pinch of dry vermouth probably would have improved the taste, and might have even passed a James Bond martini test.

He rolled their sleeping bags as tight as he could get them, tied them off, and took them out to the shed.

Cowboy and Indian had spent the night in the old shed with a rusty corrugated metal roof, yet the horses didn't look any worse for wear. The shed had acted as a wind break from the chilly night.

Fortunately, the load the horses carried was becoming lighter as they consumed water and food. Amanda wasn't much of a load for Cowboy to carry when they rode double, perhaps a hundred and five lean pounds, although a lot of that was sass. For a small person, she sure did have a mouth on her, and a loud voice.

While Chandler readied the horses, Amanda gathered up their belongings in the house, packed the cooking utensils, closed the door, and left.

Chandler saddled Cowboy and Indian and checked to make sure everything had been cinched tight. Taking the reins, he walked the horses into the yard.

The morning sun awakened the wintry land with its warm rays stretching through the bare trees. A mockingbird's melody filled the crisp air and a flock of cedar waxwings descended onto a large, thorny pyracantha bush to dine on red berries.

"Looks like the cold front pushed through," Chandler said. He squinted, checking the crystalline blue sky. Canada geese were high overhead, flying effortlessly, their muted honks drifting downward. He stood facing the east sun, soaking up the welcome warmth. "If the weather stays like this, we should be in Austin ahead of schedule."

"I can't wait," Amanda said.

She was weary of the ride, being dirty, and smelling like a horse. A proper bath with hot running water was a luxury of the past. The brief bath last night hadn't been much of a substitute. She was thankful Holly had packed two hotel sized bars of soap she had found in an empty suitcase at her ranch home. Holly told Amanda her parents must have swiped them from a hotel, tossed them in a bag, and forgotten about them. An oversight at the time, and if the soap had been found any other time, they would have been thrown out without a thought. Now it was an item worth more than a bar of gold.

Nipper had been observing Chandler and Amanda as they went about the business of packing, a clear signal he was in store for yet another long, uncomfortable ride in the makeshift side kennel.

At the sound of Amanda's high pitched whistle, Nipper pivoted to his mistress, waited for another whistle, then darted down the porch steps and ran around the yard until he found a stick. Taking it to her, he held it tight and waited for the game of tug-of-war.

"We don't have time to play," Amanda said.

Nipper, a keen observer of human body language and voice intonation, immediately recognized the deflated expression on

Amanda's face.

"Come," she ordered.

Flagrantly disobeying Amanda's instructions, Nipper didn't budge. When Amanda made a quick movement toward him he bolted to a safe spot just out of her reach. Standing in the overgrown yard, his tongue hanging out, he wagged his tail and cocked his head, looking at her with soulful eyes.

"Nipper, come," Amanda ordered. Her raised voice indicated stress and annoyance. "We're not playing. It's time to go."

While Nipper didn't understand the exact words, he did understand her tone and the fact he should obey, but he was tired of being cooped up and wanted to play. It had been a while since he had brought Amanda the spoils of his hunting. A stick would have to do for now.

A brief flash of Holly's ranch house came to Nipper and he couldn't understand why they had left the comfort of a house and the camaraderie evident among the occupants, along with the other dog known as Buster. Nipper and Buster had finally accepted each other and had become playmates.

Amanda inched toward Nipper and when she bent down to scoop him up, he darted away. It was a game he had played many times before with his mistress who normally acquiesced to his playfulness.

"I'm not playing. We have to go." Amanda's tone was stern.

Nipper only wiggled from side to side.

Amanda shrugged, turned her back to Nipper and said, "Okay, your choice. You get to walk. It'll do you good and you can burn off some energy."

Nipper observed Chandler offering a hand to Amanda, helping her onto her horse.

"Ride 'em Cowboy!" Chandler said. He prodded Cowboy with a kick in the flanks, and a few strides later, the horses and their riders disappeared beyond the tree line.

It was quiet where Nipper sat, confused. Tentatively, he looked around and tasted the air, letting the stick fall to the ground. A raccoon had trotted along the fence line, leaving a pile of scat. A musty-smelling armadillo had rooted for grubs and other worms in the yard during the night, leaving disturbed soil. A breeze brushed the trees and brown, frost-bitten leaves floated to the ground. The grass rustled and Nipper turned in that direction. The house still had scent traces of Amanda and Chandler, and Nipper gauged whether he should stay and wait. He padded up the porch stairs and stood there with hopeful eyes, scanning the road. A minute went by, then another, and Nipper was gripped with confusion.

Movement on the road!

It was Amanda and Chandler riding toward him. When Amanda whistled for Nipper, he jumped off the porch, raced through the grass, and with a mixture of relief and gleefulness he let Amanda scoop him up and put him in the carrier.

With the excitement over, he settled into the carrier and closed his eyes. The steady gait of the horse, the warmth the massive beast provided, and the comforting voices of Amanda and Chandler lulled Nipper to sleep.

* * *

The weary and cold travelers trudged on. The hours dragged on, their minds drugged from the cold and monotonous trip.

A lone coyote stood on a rise in a nearby pasture and spied them with vague curiosity before it slunk back into the dark shadows of the tree canopy lining a dry branch.

A man stooped over from carrying a large backpack walked alone on the vacant country road. He suspiciously eyed Chandler and Amanda as he neared them, giving them a wide berth without a saying a word. Nipper sensed the man's uneasiness, and when he came close, Nipper growled low in his throat, sending a clear warning to the man he wasn't wanted.

A group of two men and one woman came running up to Chandler and Amanda, begging for help, and when Chandler was forced to stop, a man tried to pull off one of their bags containing food supplies. Chandler pulled a gun and fired a warning shot, yelling, "The next shot will hit its target! So get back!"

The three dispersed.

"So many desperate people," Amanda commented. "I wish we could help them."

"We can't," Chandler said. "It's too dangerous."

The minutes droned on, hours passed.

Another day of monotonous travel came and went, lulling Amanda and Chandler into a dull routine of riding, stopping, eating, and making camp.

Clouds floated in the winter sky, a buzzard lifted off from a tree at the sight of the weary travelers. A hawk circled above, scanning the pasture for a hapless mouse or perhaps an inattentive dove.

They traveled through ghostly empty rural towns, the horses' clomping hooves echoing along the deserted streets. Merchants had boarded up the windows to their shops. Banks sat dark and empty. The plate glass window of a town's lone grocery store was a shattered mess on the sidewalk. A tourist shop had been looted of t-shirts and jams, and homemade packages of chili and cake mix. Food was obviously scarce.

Amanda and Chandler rode side by side. They were on a rarely traveled road that didn't even garner a white stripe down the middle. A truck had been pushed to the side and when Chandler passed it, he looked inside for anything useful. Finding nothing, they continued on.

Pastures segued into woodland, thick with trees and brush.

Amanda kept her eyes on the road, bored at the wearisome view. A puzzling frown spread across her face as she looked ahead. She squinted, trying to understand what she was seeing. A hundred yards ahead of them, a small, indistinguishable form was in the road.

It moved.

"Chandler, do you see that?" She pointed in the direction she was looking. "Is that a kid in the middle of the road?"

"I don't know. I've been looking at it too."

They rode closer to the form.

"It *is* a child! We have to help." Amanda kicked Indian to encourage her horse to move faster.

"Don't! Wait!" Chandler yelled.

Amanda ignored Chandler's warning. Her horse was already yards in front. He spurred Cowboy, and the horse took off running.

Amanda reined in her horse, jumped off, and went to the child. The toddler couldn't be more than eighteen months old. His face was red and wet with tears. He shivered and held out his arms to Amanda. A motherly instinct captured Amanda and she gazed upon the child with a feeling she didn't know she had.

She bent over to pick up the child. "You poor ba—"

A crowd of armed men rushed out from behind a large oak. A bullet whizzed by Chandler.

"Don't hit the horses!" one of the men yelled. "We need them and the supplies."

More shots rang out.

The toddler started screaming.

Amanda ducked and ran behind Cowboy, using him for cover. She drew her Glock and fired. The first round missed its target, while the second round caught a man in the thigh. He let out a scream and went down.

Errant bullets whizzed by.

Cowboy neighed and stomped his front hooves.

Chandler drew his Glock and in one deft motion, brought the gun up and fired a round at the closest man. He stumbled and fell backwards.

Chandler let loose another deadly round. The man went down. He popped a round straight into another guy.

"There's more coming!" Chandler yelled. "Let's get outta here!"

Amanda clambered up Cowboy, swung her leg over, and clenched her arms around Chandler's waist. "Go!"

Chandler swung Cowboy around.

Amanda emptied her gun at the crowd. When the slide on her Glock clicked back, she continued to fire, unaware the magazine was empty.

Indian was wild eyed and struggled against the riotous crowd clamoring around the horse. The crowd stripped food and water and other supplies from the horse. It was a free for all as the people crowded the horse who had been overwhelmed at the sheer amount of bodies. There was nothing Amanda or Chandler could do.

The crying child had been knocked over on his back. Stunned from the impact, the child put his thumb in his mouth, sucking on it.

Cowboy galloped away from the chaotic din, his steps heavy and solid on the road. He steadily put distance between them and the crowd, running without caution, and when they were far away, Chandler eased him into a slow trot.

"Amanda, are you okay? Are you injured?" Chandler asked.

"I'm okay," Amanda replied. "I'm a little rattled, that's all. What kind of person would use a baby as a trap?"

"Desperate people, that's who. Amanda, regardless of what you see, you have to assume it's a trap. We were living in a bubble at Holly's ranch house. We were safe, armed, and we all had each other's backs. We had food to eat and we all worked together for a goal. We worked together to survive. Out here," Chandler said, sweeping his arm to make a point, "we're strangers. We're nothing to those people who now have Indian and our extra supplies. We had what they wanted, and they were prepared to use force to take it. Including using a baby as bait. It's despicable."

"I'm sorry," Amanda said. She hung her head. "I'll be careful next time."

"There won't be a next time," Chandler said. "Not if I can help it."

CHAPTER 8

After the harrowing encounter, Amanda and Chandler had been on edge, and Cowboy was showing the strain of carrying two people, a dog, and supplies. At times, Chandler walked, giving the horse a rest.

They had left the towering pines of the East Texas Piney Woods behind, and were now entering a transition zone of the Colorado River valley with hills dotted with smaller oaks and loblolly pines where rainfall wasn't as abundant as in East Texas. By car, Austin, which was nestled in Hill Country of stunted oaks and scrubby cedars, was only an hour's drive away. By horse, another long day.

They passed a farmer tilling fertile soil using a disc plow and harrow pulled by a horse, and invented by a hardy Norwegian who had settled in the Hill Country in the 1850s. The 19th century invention was making a comeback.

"That looks like hard work," Amanda commented. The horse struggled to drag the plow, and the farmer didn't bother to look up at the passing travelers.

"Commonplace back in the 1800s," Chandler said. "I'm

guessing the farmer must have had a modern tractor that the EMP made useless.

"So this is how it's going to be?"

"Unfortunately, yes. Fortunately, the guy has land. Most aren't as lucky."

"What about your family? How do you think they are doing?"

"Considering they've got a house on the Colorado River, they should be okay. The house was an old homestead my great-grandparents settled on in the late 1880s. It still has antiques from several generations, including a Victrola."

"What's that?"

"You should know what that is," Chandler said. "Doesn't Nipper come to mind?"

"Huh?"

"The RCA Victor dog? That's who Nipper was named after, right?

"Yeah, but what's a Victrola?" Amanda asked.

"It's an old-timey record player. You have to crank it to get the turntable to spin. The needle is huge so you have to be careful. Me and my brother used to play with it when we were kids."

"It still works?"

"Yes. It doesn't need electricity. As long as you have records, it will play."

"Maybe when we get to your parents' house, we can listen to music?"

"I'll take you for a spin." Chandler said. He laughed. "Get it? Spin?"

Amanda rolled her eyes. "I get it. And yes, I'd like to go for a spin."

"I don't know about you, but I'm ready to get home."

"Me too," Amanda said. She dropped her shoulders. "I wish I had a home to go to."

"Don't be sad," Chandler said. "My parents will love you. Because if I..." Chandler trailed off before he verbally announced his private thoughts.

Amanda remained silent until curiosity got the best of her. "Because of what?"

"Nothing," Chandler said without much conviction. "My parents are great people. I know they'll love you. And you'll like my brother

Luke."

"But I'm not staying with you for long. I'm supposed to go to my great aunt's ranch."

"It's not like she's expecting you. Stay with us for a while. I'd like you to stay."

Amanda thought about what Chandler said and the underlying meaning. During their time at Holly's ranch, Chandler had never made a move on her, even though there had been plenty of opportunity for him to do so. There was a reticence about him, and for a guy of his size and the fact he was ex-military, his reluctance surprised her. From the moment she laid eyes on him in the barn when she surprised him, she had felt an immediate attraction, and she was sure he felt the same. He was a strong, capable man, one who was honest and told it like it was. They were traits she admired, and Lord knew she had been lied to by Zack. Just the thought of him made her skin crawl, and the closer she got to Austin, the more Zack was on her mind.

The trip had allowed too much time for her mind to wander, and Amanda felt as if she was a vagabond without a place to call home. After her parents had died, living with her grandfather felt like she was only marking time until her life really started. Like her life was hold. Oh sure, she had her own bedroom, and her grandfather had welcomed her with open arms, but it wasn't the same.

Thinking about her grandfather made Amanda sad, and as she thought about his death and how he died, her breathing became uneven and she blinked fast. Embarrassed by the show of emotion, she swiped under her eyes with a quick brush of the back of her hand.

With her hands wrapped around his waist, Chandler felt her uneven breathing and heard her sniffling. Even Cowboy sensed the change in her demeanor, and he adjusted his trotting to a slower, less jarring pace. Nipper raised his head out of the carrier and nosed Amanda's leg, wanting to comfort her. She scratched him behind the ears.

Trying to deflect her sadness, Chandler said, "I forgot to tell you about the house. It's not much to write home about, and is dwarfed by huge modern houses. My dad wanted to tear down the old house, but my mom didn't want to. As my mom said, their property taxes are a whole lot lower than the neighboring houses. The land is fertile, and the pecan trees are huge. Bigger than they were at Holly's place."

"Really?"

"Yes. It's the Colorado River that makes them so big. The pecans should be ripe by now. I'll make a fire in the fireplace and we'll sit around and hull pecans together. God, I can't wait to get home."

* * *

It had now been five nights of riding and six long days of being in the cold wind since Amanda and Chandler had left the comfort and safety of Holly's ranch. Weariness etched furrowed lines in the young features of her face reddened by the sun and wind. The humid conditions of East Texas relented to the dryer atmosphere of Central Texas.

An hour earlier, she had taken the reins to Cowboy as Chandler had suggested.

"It'll do you good to take the reins," he'd said. "Makes you feel like you're in control to drive." It hadn't been an entirely altruistic gesture since Chandler liked how Amanda and he fit together riding double, especially with her in front.

"How much longer to Austin?" she asked for the fourth time that day. They were coming to the end of their trip and Amanda had been asking Chandler the question as much as an impatient child would ask a parent during a long car ride.

"We'll be there tomorrow," Chandler replied.

"I'll meet your parents?"

"Yes."

"And brother?"

"Yes, why?"

"You'll see."

"What are you—"

"Hang on!" Amanda shouted.

Amanda spurred Cowboy into an all-out gallop. Caught by surprise, Chandler jerked back, holding his arms tight around Amanda's tiny waist. Amanda crouched lower and held the reins tight in her hands as Cowboy's sturdy legs gobbled more distance.

"What are you doing? You're going to get us killed!" Chandler yelled. "You need to slow down!"

Amanda ignored his protests, and hundred yards later when she drew Cowboy to a halt, Chandler was none too happy about what she had done or where she had stopped.

CHAPTER 9

"The answer is no," Chandler said. "We're not stopping here."

Amanda had seen a green highway sign advertising gas and local eateries, but it was the Packsaddle Inn Bed and Breakfast sign which caught her attention, along with the irresistible promise of *Hot Baths, Hot Food,* and *Homemade Jellies and Jams.*

At one time the Packsaddle Inn had been a stately mansion, constructed during the early 1900s by a large landowner who boasted about having the grandest house in the county.

Fast forward to when the larger ranches were divided into smaller tracts and with urban sprawl taking its toll, the Victorian style house had been converted to a bed and breakfast.

It was painted baby blue with white trimming, had a steeply pitched red roof, floor to ceiling windows, and a porch with white lattice work extending along the front part of the house. The three chimneys were made of red brick, and smoke wafted in the winter air. Several large maple trees on the property had dropped their summer foliage, leaving a carpet of rusty leaves upon the ground.

"Amanda," Chandler said pointedly, "we're not stopping here."

"We already have."

"God, you're stubborn."

Swinging her right leg over the saddle horn and taking her left foot out of the stirrup, she held onto the horn with both hands and slid down the large horse. Raising her arms over her head, she clasped her hands together and stretched, leaning to one side, then the other. When finished, she unzipped Nipper's carrier, picked him up, and set him on the ground.

Nipper sniffed the air, his wet nose twitching, taking in the smell of a feral cat hiding in the dense foliage of a large dormant azalea bush near the house. Meat cooking over a backyard grill piqued his interest and stimulated his saliva glands. An unusual smell drifted along a languid air current and Nipper's mind whirled trying to identify the odd odor. It required further investigation, but when he went in that direction Amanda raced after him and tapped him on his rump. She said a firm, "No," followed by "Stay." Nipper obeyed and sat on his haunches, waiting for instruction.

The unusual odor lingered.

Nipper raised his nose in the air, sniffing. The odor worried him. He had never smelled it before and his mind whirled trying to place it, dismissing each memory associated with different odors that his world consisted of. It wasn't an animal. Possibly human, but it smelled off. It was something different…something that definitely aroused his curiosity.

"We can't stay," Chandler said. "If this place was so popular don't you think there'd be more people here? We're the only ones. Don't you think that's odd?"

Amanda put her hands on her hips and challenged Chandler. "No, I don't think it's odd. How would they be able to get the word out? Can't exactly advertise on the internet, can they?"

"We're still not—"

Amanda waved him off. "I'm hungry, we've lost our supplies, I haven't had a bath in days, and I look and smell like something the cat dragged in. Or rather the dog in my case." She tapped Nipper to get his attention.

Nipper cocked his head and looked at her quizzically. Sensing her displeasure, he sunk to the ground, his nose still twitching, trying to identify the odor.

"That's right," she said, pointing her finger at him. "No more

58

bringing dead animals to me. Chandler, I'm not meeting your family like this. I've got a week's worth of grime under my nails. My hair looks like crap, and I haven't seen a mirror in a week, so there's no telling what's on my face."

"They won't care. I promise you," he said.

"We're staying, and that's all there is to it."

"For such a small girl—"

"I'm not a girl. I'm a woman and I can shoot a Glock as well as you do."

"No, you can't."

"Really? Maybe we should have a shoot off," Amanda shot back.

"Like a dance off, but with Glocks?"

"You betcha."

"That would be a waste of ammo. Besides, you'd lose."

"No I wouldn't."

"I'll give you credit," Chandler said, shaking his head, "for as small as you are you sure do have a lot of sass."

"Dynamite comes in small packages," Amanda reminded him. "You haven't seen the half of it!"

"I'd hate to see what happened if anybody lit your fuse."

"I'd blow up. That's what I'd do."

"I have no doubt about that." Chandler chuckled at the thought. He paused and thought quickly. "If it makes you feel better, I'll be sure my family doesn't meet you until you've had a chance to clean up. So get Nipper and come on back. Deal?"

Before Amanda had time to protest, an elderly man hobbled down the porch stairs. He held onto the handrail while steadying himself with a cane. "I'm Walter," he said in a gravelly voice. "Welcome. You've come to the right place if you're looking for a hot bath and a meal." He ran a hand through his full head of white hair. "This here is my wife, Eve."

An equally elderly woman came out to greet Amanda and Chandler. She wiped her hands on a colorful apron and smoothed down her graying hair tied into a bun. She smiled pleasantly.

"I'm Chandler and this is Amanda," Chandler said.

"Nice to meet you," Walter said. "We haven't had many travelers lately, and business has been slow. Glad you folks stopped."

Amanda sidled up to Chandler sitting atop Cowboy. She whispered, "They're harmless. I'm going on in. Come with me." She batted her eyelashes twice and smiled as innocent as a baby Easter bunny.

"We'll talk later." Chandler's voice was gruff. "I need to teach you some things about safety."

"Oh. I think I could teach *you* some things."

Chandler recognized Amanda was challenging him, again, but now was not the time to get into an argument. "How much do you charge for a meal and a bath?" he asked the old man.

"Reasonable rates," the old man said. "What do you have to trade? Paper money is no good right now."

"What about silver dollars?"

Walter rubbed the stubble on his chin, thinking. "Silver dollars, you say? How many you got?"

The question raised red flags, and since Chandler prided himself on not lying, he decided to throw out a question. "Make me an offer."

"How about four?"

"No can do. Two's my offer."

The old man spied him with interest. "You won't find anything better than this between here and Austin. Tell you what. I'll meet you halfway. I'll take three silver dollars."

"That's fair enough," Chandler said. He handed over three of his ten silver dollars, irritated at the extravagance and wasting time on something so frivolous as a bath and a hot meal. He should have gone hunting, but it was too late for should've or could've. He decided to have a talk with Amanda about safety measures after she cleaned up.

"Thank you," Walter said. He dropped the silver dollars into his shirt pocket. "You kids come on in." With a wave of his hand, he motioned for Amanda and Chandler to follow him.

Eve went to Amanda and put her arm around her, bringing her close. In an endearing grandmotherly voice she said, "Dear, come on in. We'll get you cleaned up in a bit. I've got two granddaughters who will fuss over you just like if you were in a fancy spa. Let me see your hands."

Amanda tentatively held out her hands, embarrassed at her ragged nails and scraped and calloused palms.

"Oh dear," Eve said. She put a hand to her cheek. "No man wants to see hands like those. You haven't had a manicure in a long time, have you?"

"No, ma'am."

"My granddaughters can give you a manicure and paint your nails. Your husband will like that."

"He's not my husband," Amanda said, somewhat embarrassed.

"Boyfriend?"

"He's escorting me to my great aunt's ranch near Austin."

"That sure is nice of him. He seems like a nice and capable man."

Eve glanced at Chandler. He had dismounted Cowboy and was retrieving his LaRue rifle. Eve noted the rifle was no ordinary gun. She recognized it as an AR type, but the folded down sights and peculiar cylinder type forearm stood out as unusual. Although the scope brand of Leupold meant nothing to her, she recognized the quick detachable mount indicating the rifle could serve many purposes. The flawless finish, the chromed bolt carrier, and the flashhider with external threading convinced her the rifle was not the rifle of an ordinary man.

When Chandler caught Eve looking at him, she smiled demurely and dropped her gaze.

"Are you hungry?" she asked.

Chandler eyed her suspiciously. "I could eat."

"I just made hot stew," Eve said in her most unthreatening voice. "And I've got jalapeno cornbread in the cast iron skillet. Made it over coals a little while ago."

"I love cornbread," Amanda said, butting in. "I haven't had a hot meal in days."

As they were walking up the front porch steps, two teenaged girls, petite like Amanda and younger by about five years, making them around fifteen or sixteen, skipped down the staircase.

"These are my granddaughters," Eve said. "Megan and Brandy. Girls, say hi to Amanda."

The girls walked past Amanda without making eye contact. One mumbled, "Nice to meet you."

Eve said, "Girls, put the horse with the mule that's already in the barn and put out some feed for them. When you're finished get the tub ready for our guest. And be sure to warm up the pump house so it's not so chilly in there."

61

Megan, older than Brandy by one year replied, "Yes, ma'am."

"Wait," Amanda said. "My dog. Can he come in?"

"Sorry, honey," Eve said. "I don't allow dogs in the house while we eat. He'll be just fine outside. I'll make him a nice bed on the porch. Is that alright?"

"He's completely housetrained and won't beg for food."

Eve shook her head. "No dogs. I'll be sure his bed is comfortable."

"Alright," Amanda sighed. "Thank you."

Nipper had followed Amanda up to the front porch. When the door opened, he tried to wiggle in, to which Amanda said, "Sorry, boy. You can't come in." She scooted him aside with her foot. "Stay."

"Chandler," Eve called, "come on in."

"I'll be there in a minute."

Chandler's eyes swept over the Packsaddle compound. Two trucks and several cars sat idle under the canopy of a large oak which he estimated to be about two hundred years old. An old tractor sat idle, rimmed by annual flowers that had withered and gone to seed. Pine trees loomed skyward, and pine needles carpeted the ground. The inn was on the boundary of the area of Texas known as the Lost Pines, a swath of land where the soil conditions were optimum for pine trees thought to be descendants of a great forest from the Ice Age.

To the right of the inn, coals glowed in a fire pit over which a large cast iron pot was suspended. Past that there was another shed. The two teenaged girls brushed past Chandler without so much as a "hello", then disappeared into the pump house. After a moment they emerged, each holding a pot, went to the fire pit, and proceeded to fill the pots with hot water.

Chandler slung his LaRue rifle over his shoulder.

Nipper looked at him hopefully.

"Sorry, boy. You can't come in." Chandler reached out to the dog and stroked him along the ruff on his back, and gave him a quick scratch behind his ears. "As soon as we get to my house, you'll have the run of it, and the softest bed you can imagine."

* * *

Chandler walked into the house and shut the door. Standing on the porch, Nipper waited, his tail thumping, hopeful the door would swing open and he'd be invited in.

At first glance Nipper seemed harmless, and his cute face belied the fact he was a successful hunter and could be ferocious when called upon. As a country dog, he had presented Amanda with the spoils of his hunting prowess, and many times had waited for a pat on the head or other gesture indicating approval. Instead he was met with a scolding tone that had only solidified his desire to bring a trophy which would be met with the respect he so craved. He had brought her the lifeless bodies of small woodland animals including a rabbit, a squirrel, a gopher, a rat from the barn, even various birds, although none garnered the praise he desired.

He was a mixture of a Jack Russell terrier and several other medium sized indistinguishable breeds which coalesced into thirty-five pounds of intelligent feistiness. Named due to his resemblance to the RCA Victor dog, which was thought to be part bull terrier, the bloodline most likely accounted for Nipper's well-muscled frame and protective nature. He could be placid at times, yet fiercely loyal, and considered Amanda his mistress. He would protect her with his life if needed.

Nipper had sensed Chandler was now part of his pack, and he gradually came to trust and respect this new member.

Nipper cocked his head and waited, listening to unfamiliar voices inside the house. Chandler had not participated in the conversation. When Amanda laughed, Nipper perked up his ears at the sound of her voice. After a moment, he moved closer to the door and nosed the crack, listening and smelling.

The older woman's voice rose in a questioning intonation, and when Chandler responded it had been gruff.

A chair squeaked and Chandler's footfalls were heavy on the wood floor. A terse exchange followed between Amanda and Chandler, the meaning of it lost among the muffled voices.

Then it was quiet until a casual conversation started.

Various cooking aromas wafted out through the crack in the front door and onto the porch. Nipper sat on his haunches staring at the front door. Silverware and dishes clinked on the table, and he thumped his tail in anticipation of a tidbit of food.

Minutes went by.

UNKNOWN WORLD

The feral cat dashed out from its hiding place near the house and Nipper forgot about being locked outside when his chase instinct captured him. The hunter within the white dog with patches of black on his fur leapt down the stairs, skittered across the dry grass, racing after the gray cat.

The wily cat ran low to the ground, dashed under the barbed wire fence, and scrambled into the thick woods, dark with leaf litter and moist soil.

Nipper bolted to the fence and belly crawled under it. A barb pinched him and he let out a surprised yelp. He nosed the ground following the cat, maneuvering around a large tree covered in vines, skirted various patches of brush, and after a while he came to a stop, sniffing the air.

That odd odor which had piqued his interest earlier filled the air with a pungent smell, and a curiosity which his ancestors had passed down to their descendants was as strong in Nipper as it was in his wolf forbearers.

The cat no longer interested Nipper, so he changed directions letting his nose guide him closer to where the odor emanated from.

He followed a short path carved out by countless trips of four legged animals, crossed over a seasonal creek bed, and came to where the earth had been disturbed. The unusual odor filled his nostrils and instinct guided him to dig.

At first Nipper pawed tentatively at the loosened earth, testing the hardness. He put his nose to the earth and huffed a warm breath. Unsatisfied this was the optimum spot he needed to dig, he changed directions, nosed the ground again, then dug with vigor.

Dirt flew in all directions.

His paws and nose became caked with the dark soil, still he dug faster, more intently, until his paws felt a change in the soil. He stood back and blinked the dirt away from his eyes and huffed the soil from his nose.

He panted and his tongue hung to one side, dripping droplets of drool.

When he spied the object of his intentions, the odor came full and strong and he cocked his head, looking at it curiously. Like a person visually recognizing objects, Nipper's mind filed through his catalogued odors associated with the respective object.

This one was different.

64

It was new.

Finally, Amanda would be proud of him.

He dug and bit, pulling at the object until a piece broke off that was small enough for him to carry. Taking it in his mouth he backtracked the path he had taken until he came to the house.

Nipper cocked his head, listening for Amanda. He lifted his snout, tasting the air. An aroma similar to ones of the shower, full of shampoo and soap at his old house, came to him.

His wet nose twitched.

Amanda's scent mingled among the extraneous odors he dismissed as not being important or needing further investigation. Voices carried in the still air, and when he recognized Amanda's voice he padded to the pump house.

He would present her with his trophy and she would say, "Good dog!"

CHAPTER 10

Chandler walked into the house and immediately noticed a lingering odor of fresh paint. To his left and on the other side of the large dining table was a white sheet cordoning off another room.

Eve directed Amanda and Chandler to sit at the dining room table big enough to seat twelve people. It was in the middle of the room, which was just to the left of the foyer.

"Amanda," Eve said, "you sit here in case I need you to help me in the kitchen. You won't have to crawl over everybody. Chandler, it would be best for you to sit to the right of Amanda. That way if we get any more visitors you won't have your back to them. You can see them as they walk in."

"You want me to sit next to the sheet?" Chandler asked.

"If you don't mind."

"Can I look in there?"

"Absolutely. Go right ahead."

Chandler pushed the sheet to the side and peeked in. Opaque plastic drop cloths covered the furniture. A paint roller and paint brush had been placed next to a can of paint.

"We put the sheet there because we're painting the room, and don't want our visitors to be inconvenienced with the mess."

Chandler took a seat at the table.

"No guns allowed at the table." Eve held out her hands. "If you don't mind, I'll take your rifle and put it in another room."

"I do mind," Chandler said. "It's staying with me."

"Christopher Chandler!" Amanda said. "We're guests here. Didn't your mother teach you manners?"

Chandler flashed Amanda an angry expression. "She taught me a lot of things. My father too, as did the military, one of which was not to give your weapon up."

"Be polite and give it to her," Amanda ordered.

"I'll just leave then," Chandler said tersely. He rose from the table.

Amanda scooted back from her chair, nearly hitting the wall.

Eve said, "Oh dear, please don't squabble over the rifle. You don't need to leave. We haven't had guests in so long, and I'd hate for you to have a bad impression of us. I have so much food. Won't you stay? Please?"

"I'll put it here in the corner," Chandler said, "and that's as far out of my reach as it will be."

Amanda opened her mouth to say something then thought better of it. She sat back down, glanced at Chandler, and said a terse, "Thank you."

* * *

"Eve," Amanda said, "the meal was delicious." She dabbed the sides of her mouth with a napkin, folded it, and set it on the table. She placed the spoon she had been using on top of the napkin. "Thank you so much."

"You're welcome. Would you like another helping?"

"No, ma'am. I'm full, but Chandler might like another helping." Amanda glanced at Chandler.

"Of course," Eve said.

Eve ladled another helping of stew into his bowl. Chandler's eyes went to the bowl. "I definitely could eat more."

"Wonderful," Eve said. "It's so nice to prepare food for those who appreciate it and who have a hearty appetite. Walter and I don't eat much."

"Can I help you with the dishes?" Amanda asked.

"Not at all, honey. Walter and I will clear the table. Let's get you cleaned up and then you and your friend can be on your way before it gets dark. My granddaughters should have gotten your bath nice and hot by now. The pump house is on the side of the house. You can't miss it. And please shut the door on the way out. Don't need to let in any more drafty air. Stay as long as you want to. The tub water will stay warm for about an hour."

"I won't be that long," Amanda said. "See you in a little while."

Eve escorted Amanda to the front door. She shut the door then stepped over to the window and waited until Amanda had entered the pump house. Megan popped her head out and waved once in the direction of the main house. Eve locked the deadbolt.

While Chandler was busy eating his second helping, and now that Amanda was out of sight, Eve strolled over to the dining room. She glanced in the direction of the sheet separating the dining room from the room being painted. She made a slight motion of her head, so inconspicuous and seemingly natural that when Chandler lifted his eyes, he didn't notice the motion.

"Chandler," Eve said, "would you mind helping me to take down the sheet? It looks so tacky and I'd like to get the room ready for our next guests. The paint should be dry by now, and my grandsons are out somewhere hunting." She rubbed her hands. "My arthritis flares up in this cold weather."

"Sure, I'll help," Chandler said. Rising from the table, he walked over to the sheet, reached up, and removed one of the tacks. Holding one end high, he stepped to the other side and removed the remaining tack. The room appeared just as he saw it earlier. A painter's tarp was on the floor, and drop cloths covered the furniture. An empty bucket of paint sat to the side.

"I'll help you fold that," Eve said. She positioned herself so that Chandler had to put his back to the room being painted in order to face her.

Holding both ends high above his head, he walked it over to her. Eve sidestepped away from him.

Chandler said, "The paint job looks—"

The force of a shovel hitting his head stunned Chandler so much that he didn't have time to react or to make a defensive move, reach for his Glock, or yell a warning to Amanda. He teetered on wobbly legs, his eyes rolled up into his head, and he thought of Amanda and how small and vulnerable she was, and how he wouldn't be able to help her.

The sheet fell to the ground.

His last image was of Eve standing over him.

His last thought before he lost consciousness was he was going to kill Eve even if he had to do it with his bare hands.

* * *

"Mama, what do you want me to do with him?" A large man, fiftyish, probably around three hundred pounds, stood over Chandler. He set the shovel up against the wall.

Eve's warm and grandmotherly facade switched off like a light switch. Her voice was condescending when she said, "What do you think, Bruno?"

"I don't know, Mama." Bruno picked at something in his scalp, looked at it, then flicked it away.

"For God's sake get rid of him. And don't leave the shovel in here. It's dirty and I just cleaned this place." Eve knelt down and went through Chandler's pockets. She found the remaining silver dollars and some cash, then stripped him of his Glock and extra magazines. She patted him down, feeling for extra weapons. She found a knife in the front side pocket of his pants and tossed it aside.

"I could bash his head in right here," Bruno offered.

"And get blood all over my floor and new paint? What's wrong with you?"

"Sorry, Mama. I wasn't thinkin'."

"As usual," Eve said. "Walter! Come over here and you two drag this man outside. You can kill him however you see fit, then get rid of the body. The girl too. She's got a gold pocket watch, so be sure to get that. Now that I think about it, throw Chandler in the shed and get the horse out of sight. We don't want anyone nosing around here asking questions where we got the horse."

"Yes, Mama."

CHAPTER 11

A northerly wind had picked up, blowing leaves around. Amanda estimated it was mid-afternoon. She hurriedly walked to the pump house, thankful she had a full belly, and for once she wasn't cold to the bone. With food being rationed, it had been a long time since she had finished a meal without still being hungry.

Chandler had been so wrong about this place, and once they were back on the road, she'd have a talk with him about trusting people. After finding his girlfriend in bed with his best friend, Amanda supposed he had a right to be distrusting. Things were different, times were different now, and he needed to get over it. Amanda wasn't anything like his previous girlfriend. Hadn't she proved that? Gradually, they had gotten to know each other, and Amanda liked what she had learned about him. He would be what her mother referred to as, "A good catch."

She'd work on reeling in the prized fish later. For now, it was bath time.

She yawned, aware of just how weary and tired she was. A hot bath would be a luxury and she couldn't wait to soak in the tub.

UNKNOWN WORLD

The pump house was a rectangular building about the size of a bedroom, with curtained windows on each side and cement steps leading to the door. Amanda opened the door and walked in, greeted with the aroma of scented candles and a full bath. She put her hand in the opaque water, bubbly with soap. Rising steam curled in the air.

Megan and Brandy sat on chairs placed to the side. Megan had her legs crossed and was tapping her right foot impatiently. They stopped talking when Amanda walked in.

"We're ready for you," Megan said. Rising, she went to the door, stuck her head out and waved.

Before she shut the door, an odd noise came from the main house, a clanging sound, then something akin to a piece of furniture being dropped.

"What was that?" Amanda asked.

Megan's eyes darted to Brandy. She shook her head, an increment so small Amanda failed to see it. Megan dismissed Amanda's question with a wave of her hand. She shut the door. "They're painting or moving furniture, that's all. Grandma said she needed to get the room ready for guests."

Amanda accepted this explanation without question.

"You can put your clothes on the chair. We won't look."

While Megan and Brandy had their backs to Amanda, she disrobed and placed her clothes on the back of the chair. She tested the temperature of the water with a toe. It was hot, not too hot, rather just right for a bath. She slipped into the deep tub, scooting her feet to the end until the water covered her up to her décolletage. She acclimated quickly to the water.

The milky-looking water provided ample coverage for the modest guest, and soon the warm water and cozy atmosphere lulled Amanda into complacency, and to a place just short of sleep. She draped both her hands over the bathtub rim while the teenaged girls primped and lotioned her calloused hands.

"Ready for a shampoo?" Megan asked.

Amanda nodded.

"Scoot down a little more and get your hair wet."

Amanda submerged her head underwater."

In a low voice, Megan asked, "Are we ready yet?"

"No," Brandy whispered. "Grandma said to wait for Bruno."

Amanda lifted her head from under the water and Megan instructed Brandy to shampoo her hair. Strong fingers massaged Amanda's scalp starting at the temples then working backward to the nape of her neck. Amanda rolled with the strokes.

"That feels nice," Amanda commented.

"Time to rinse," Brandy said.

Amanda closed her eyes and submerged again, working the shampoo out of her hair. Rising, she sat and blinked the water out of her eyes. Megan and Brandy flanked her on both sides of the bathtub and they were looking at her oddly.

"What's going on?" Amanda asked.

"Nothing. We're just going to leave you here for a—"

A scratch at the door caught everyone's attention. Another scratch sounded, followed by a whimper.

"That's Nipper," Amanda said. "He wants in. Can you let him in?"

Megan opened the door a crack to let Nipper in. He padded into the small space, wagging his tail, sidled over to the tub, and dropped what looked like a chewed-on animal.

"Oh, Nipper! That's so gross!" Amanda said, exasperated. "What kind of dead animal do you have this time?" She pinched her nose shut. "That smells!" She turned her attention to Megan and Brandy, who had stepped closer to Nipper. "I'm sorry. If you can hand me a towel, I'll take that out of here."

Brandy and Megan exchanged worried glances. Amanda's eyes fell to the item Nipper had dragged in. It was nearly a foot long, slender at both ends. The skin was black and mottled and had five appendages that looked like...fingers.

"Is that a...you brought me a...is that a *human hand*?" Amanda's gaze shifted from Megan to Brandy. "What kind of place is—"

With the speed of a striking snake, Megan rushed Amanda and pushed her head under the soapy water. Amanda only had time to close her mouth before she was violently pushed underwater. She struggled in the slippery tub and lashed out at Megan with her fists.

Water sloshed over the sides.

Nipper barked and growled.

Brandy grabbed one of Amanda's flailing hands, trying to control her. Their matching strength made it difficult.

Amanda kicked and struggled and when her mouth breached the

water, she took a gulp of air and opened her eyes to assess the situation. Brandy squeezed down hard on Amanda's head and tried pushing her back under water. Using her legs like scissors, Amanda twisted her lower body, throwing it up and out of the water like a Phoenix rising. She clenched her legs around Brandy's waist, and hooked her feet together at the ankles.

Brandy tumbled into the tub.

Soapy water spilled over the tub and onto the floor, making it slippery.

Nipper snapped and growled, biting at Megan's ankle, darting like a mongoose attacking a cobra.

Megan still had a firm grip on Amanda's hair. She kicked at Nipper and missed. He darted around until he latched onto her ankle, clamped hard, and bit with wild abandon, drawing blood through her jeans. He shook her leg like it was an animal he was trying to kill.

Megan, now distracted by her throbbing ankle, let go of Amanda. She hopped on one leg, trying to shake off the dog. She hit him with her fists, yet Nipper refused to relinquish his hold on her.

The muscled dog thrashed her leg back and forth, causing Megan to lose her balance. She fell over, hitting her head on the side of the porcelain tub. She landed with a thud on the concrete floor, momentarily stunned. She feebly tried to get up.

Nipper jumped on her and went for the neck, biting into the soft flesh, tearing at it. Blood gushed out, and Megan's hands went to her neck.

With the weight off her head, Amanda flipped Brandy over onto her stomach, forcing her face down into the tub. Straddling her, Amanda clasped her arm around her neck. Taking her left hand, she held onto her right elbow, tightening the grasp.

Brandy fought and clawed, kicking furiously. Water got into her nose and mouth and she sputtered and coughed.

For several long minutes, Amanda held Brandy underwater until she fought no more and her hands fell listlessly to her sides.

Breathing hard, Amanda let go of Brandy and sat back in the tub. Adrenaline pulsed through her and she glanced around, afraid someone else might be coming after her. She was keenly aware of her vulnerability and her state of undress. She glanced at Megan, sprawled flat on the floor, her eyes open. A river of blood poured out of her neck and onto the concrete floor.

Stepping out of the tub, she quickly towel dried herself, threw on her jeans, shirt, socks, and boots. Opening the satchel, she breathed a sigh of relief. Her Glock 19 was still there.

Nipper stood over Megan's lifeless body. He was panting hard and had a wild look in his eyes. Blood covered his snout and neck.

"Nipper, come here boy. Did they hurt you? Let me see." Amanda let her hands roam over Nipper, feeling his legs and sides for any wounds. Finding none, she took a washcloth and dipped it in the tub. Using purposeful strokes, she cleaned the blood from his fur.

Nipper stood patiently while Amanda washed off the blood. When she was finished, he nosed the floor, sniffing all around. When he found the hand, he latched onto it and presented it to Amanda.

She didn't know whether to laugh or cry. "No. It's still gross. Drop it."

Reluctantly, Nipper let the hand fall to the floor.

"Oh, no," Amanda whispered. Her thoughts went to Chandler and how right he had been about this place. She should have listened to him. If he knew what was going on, he would have helped her by now. He must be in trouble.

"Nipper," she said, "we have to help Chandler."

CHAPTER 12

Chandler woke and blinked his eyes into focus. He was surprised he was still alive. A throbbing pain on the back of his head had roused him from sleep. Self-preservation guided him to be still and not move in case he was being watched.

With his muzzy head rapidly clearing, he assessed his situation, determining he was on a dirt floor in some kind of outdoor shed, possibly the one he'd seen earlier.

The shed was quite solid. The walls were made of two by twelves solidly nailed to each stud. The wooden door was two inches thick, secured by a stout, rusty chain. Without an axe, Chandler would have to wait for one of his captors to open the door.

He now understood the lack of interaction the two teenaged girls showed him meant they were part of the insidious plan and had known all along their time was limited. There was no telling how many wayward travelers had met an untimely demise at this evil place.

Amanda.

She had virtually no chance against the trap set for them.

Chandler realized how much he had come to know and respect her. She was a pistol. Quick witted, brave, and she had shown grit at her grandpa's house when the man stormed the house. It took guts to kill a grown man with only evil on his mind. Chandler closed his eyes and said a quick prayer to the Almighty to keep her safe.

He was a man of quiet faith, who lived by an unwavering code of honor. He was a firm believer that the good guys would win and the bad guys would lose, although it didn't mean there wouldn't be casualties or injuries in the process of winning. Chandler wasn't one to back away from overwhelming odds, and as of now, the odds weren't stacked in his favor.

One way or the other, people were going to get hurt here or killed.

He gained an inner strength and fortitude after saying a prayer to the Almighty. It steeled him for what he knew was coming.

His hands were bound behind his back, and from the hard plastic cutting into his wrists, no doubt zip ties had been used. He had been gagged, and when he breathed out through his nose, dry dust blew around his face.

His lips were parched, and he became aware of his thirst.

It was dark and musty in the shed, and he got a whiff of an odd odor emanating from the floor. He sniffed, trying to place the smell. It was like smelling dried blood. Yes, that was it. People had been killed here, probably right where he was, and had bled out on the floor.

The only light source was a translucent piece of corrugated fiberglass placed near the center of the corrugated sheet metal roof. A redneck skylight, and a cheap one at that.

Now that he was coming to his senses, he realized he was cold and was missing his jacket. His belt had been removed, along with his Glock and extra magazines. Whoever had put him in here wouldn't have left his Glock anywhere near him.

His eyes gradually acclimated to the darkness.

He stayed as still as possible.

Determining he was alone, he wiggled his hands until his fingers could reach the inside of his pants near the small of his back. He searched for the duct tape he had placed there before the trip started. He worked the duct tape until it loosened enough for him to locate the finger ring seatbelt cutter he had taped to his waistband. He was thankful he had taken the extra precaution before he left on the trip. Stretching his index finger, he wiggled it into place, and it was a simple matter to pull the cutter free of the tape and get to work.

The miniscule blade, similar to a gut hook portion of a skinning knife, pulled through the plastic zip ties as if they were made of butter. Shaking off the zip ties, Chandler massaged his hands and wrists to regain circulation. He ripped off the gag.

He stood and the throbbing in his head sounded like drums beating to the rhythm of a rock song. He leaned against a wall to steady himself. He touched his head and palpated his scalp, inspecting it.

He had a large knot on the back of his head. The blood had caked, so at least he wasn't bleeding anymore.

He needed a weapon, and there had to be something of use in the shed. He spied buckets, jars, and personal items such as belts and shoes. Taking one of the belts, he looped it on. Digging around in a box, he found a pair of trousers, tossed those aside, then saw a jacket. Holding it up, he estimated it would fit. He shrugged it on, and when he did, he noticed an old number 10 can full of coins, jewelry, some paper money, and several wedding bands. He looked at it oddly.

"What kind of shithole is this?" Chandler's expression was one of horror and utter disgust as he realized the scope of this operation.

The old man and woman pretended to be harmless so they could kill unsuspecting travelers and strip them of anything valuable. The old man had been clever at not taking paper money, and Chandler had fallen for the ruse, hook, line, and sinker. Trading a hot meal and a bath for silver dollars? Who would have suspected two benevolent acting inn owners to be the caretakers of the devil's playground?

Taking another look around the shed, he tossed aside several boxes filled with clothes and his hope shot up when he found an old Coleman fuel can without a top. Wedged in the corner of the shed, the can was filled to the brim with pocket knives. Not only were the owners of the Packsaddle Inn evil, they were also sloppy.

Obviously they had forgotten about the stash of knives.

Bad for them, good for Chandler.

A Kershaw similar to the one he had was on top of the pile. Chandler clipped it to his back pocket then selected six pocket knives with the longest blades he could find. Opening them, he carefully placed the handles of three knives between his fingers of each hand and made a tight fist. He swung up and fast, testing the viability of his new weapon. Hugh Jackman's character Wolverine in the movie *X-Men* came to mind.

Heavy footsteps approached.

Chandler quickly positioned himself behind the door where he could melt into the dark shadows.

The door swung open and a large man, possibly topping three hundred pounds with a belly to match, stood there with a meat cleaver positioned high over his head. He shut the door and squinted in the darkness, searching for his prey. Like a cat toying with an injured mouse, he said, "Come to Papa."

With lightening fast speed, Chandler jumped out from the shadows and shoved a fistful of knives into the man's armpit, severing vital nerves and tendons.

The man stumbled back and the meat cleaver tumbled out of his hand.

Without missing a beat, Chandler shoved another fistful of knives into the man's throat, jamming them upward, twisting the knives ninety degrees to ensure the last three cut as many blood vessels as possible.

The fat man stumbled back and clutched his throat. The man had a surprised look on his face and was unable to vocalize his pain or shout a warning. Blood bubbled out of his throat each time he exhaled. Inhaling, all he got was a mouthful of blood. With his life pouring out of him, he wobbled and clumsily fell face down to the floor, his neck hemorrhaging a copious amount of blood.

Chandler stood over the man and waited.

It didn't take long for the cuts from the Wolverine-inspired knives to finish the man off.

Working quickly, Chandler retrieved the old GI 1911 the man had shoved in the back of his pants, along with a fully-loaded magazine in one of his pockets. A quick glance determined the 45 was not in optimum shape. It rattled when he shook it and the finish was scratched and rusted. Regardless, it was a last resort weapon that could save Amanda.

Finding the 1911 chamber empty, he jacked a round into the chamber, flipped the safety upward, then inserted the full magazine to bring the pistol to full capacity. Chandler stuffed the 1911 into his

front right waistband. He placed the other magazine in his pocket.
Time to find Amanda.

CHAPTER 13

Chandler opened the shed door a crack and peered outside. The view only gave him a slit of his surroundings, so he swiveled his gaze to the other side, taking in as much as possible. The main house was straight in front of the shed, possibly thirty yards away. Sprinting to the house through open land without any cover would only get him a bullet. The pump house where Amanda had taken a bath was to his far left, out of sight.

He opened the door another inch.

It was quiet, with only the sounds of the country filling the bleak loneliness. The wind whistled through the trees and a dark cloud hovered overhead. A sprinkling of rain fell, dampening the land, bringing with it the peculiar smell of rain. A crow cawed somewhere in the distance.

He thought he heard Nipper barking, but couldn't be sure. The sound was too muddled.

He needed to get out of the shed and find cover. If he became trapped, it would be the end of him, and Amanda would be next. He vaguely remembered a metal burn barrel large enough in circumference to conceal him. He opened the door only wide enough for him to squeeze through, then keeping his back to the shed he hugged the sides and dashed behind it.

Bullets whizzed by him, striking the dirt.

Chandler flinched, then quickly pivoted to the other side of the shed. He crouched low, trying to make himself as small as possible, not exactly an easy feat considering his six foot one frame. His eyes darted to the woods behind the shed and beyond, trying to determine who was using him as target practice.

He brought up the 1911.

"You're mine now." It was Eve.

If Eve was trying to flush him out, she'd have to do better than that. He decided to turn the tables on her.

"I'm hurt!" Chandler yelled, cupping a hand to his mouth. "And I don't have my guns."

"You expect me to believe that?"

"I don't lie. Never have, never will. I came here with my LaRue and a Glock, which I don't have now, so don't shoot." Technically, it was the truth. Someone *had* taken his sniper rifle and his favorite semi-automatic pistol.

Eve laughed. "That's right, I heard you say earlier you don't lie, something about priding yourself on always telling the truth."

Eve's voice sounded like it was nearer to Chandler. Her yelling had turned to the inflection of a normal voice being projected at a casual level.

"Where's Bruno?" Eve asked.

While Chandler had expected Eve to try to sneak up behind him from the other side of the shed, she had done the opposite of what he expected. His back was to her and at this range, she couldn't miss.

Her problem was she didn't expect Chandler to be armed.

He whipped around and fired the 1911 directly at her chest. The force of the bullet knocked her backwards and she crumpled to the ground.

Chandler went to her, put his foot on her wrist, and pried his Glock from the old woman's hand. He looked at her for a moment, and momentarily felt sorry for her. Like, about a second of feeling sorry.

Her breathing was labored and her eyes glassy. She only had minutes to live before the life drained out of her. "I thought you said you weren't armed," she mumbled.

"I said I don't have my guns. That was the truth. This," Chandler said, showing her the 1911, "is the fat man's gun. He won't be needing it anymore."

"You bastard," Eve spat. "That was my son."

"Too bad. Bruno's with Satan now, where you're going. When you see Bruno, tell him I'm sorry he couldn't stick around."

Eve looked at him, puzzled.

"He'll understand."

She took a shallow breath, her eyes fluttered, and she exhaled slowly. It was the last breath she ever took.

CHAPTER 14

Amanda crouched low, squatting on her heels in the dark woods behind the Packsaddle Inn, Nipper by her side. Pine needles blanketed the ground. She double checked her Glock 19. It had one round in the chamber plus fifteen in the magazine. The other fully loaded magazine was in her satchel she had slung across her chest.

She peeked out from behind the pine tree where she had taken cover. She had a good line of sight to the Packsaddle Inn and the pump house where she had nearly lost her life. Scanning the area, she saw no movement. Cowboy and a mule were eating hay in the stable. Cowboy intermittently looked around, and Amanda noticed his skittish behavior. Not only was he a strong horse, he was smart. The horse sensed something wasn't right.

There was movement at the house and Amanda lowered herself to the ground. Nipper growled.

"Shhh!" Amanda put a finger to her lips and looked straight at Nipper. "Shhh. We have to be quiet," she whispered.

* * *

Walter ambled out of the house and stood on the back porch. "Kyle," he said to his youngest grandson, "you run as fast as you can about halfway to the pump house. Take cover behind the old tractor. You'll be safe there."

"Okay, Grandpa," Kyle said. "I've got your back."

"Trevor," Walter said. "I want you to be our backup and hide in the woods where you have a clear shot. It's about a hundred yards from there to where I think Chandler is. Once we flush him out, you take him down with his own rifle."

"Okay, Grandpa."

* * *

Amanda observed the men exit the house then stop to talk before scattering. Walter hobbled over to a car parked to the side of the Inn. With great effort, he knelt on one knee.

The youngest grandson took cover behind a tractor, but it was the tallest one who worried her the most. He sprinted away from the others, back to the woods, selected a tree to hide behind, directly in her line of sight. Small saplings and undergrowth dotted the land between her and the rifle he held, which appeared strikingly similar to Chandler's.

It *was* his rifle, and they planned to use it to kill him.

Swiveling her gaze back to the compound, she saw Chandler inching his way along a shed. She wanted to scream out to him that it was a trap, but if she did, she'd give away her location. As of now, that was about her only trump card. Nobody knew she was there.

A round blasted dirt in front of Chandler and he dove for cover behind a burn barrel.

Amanda immediately recognized his perilous position and watched the horrifying scene from a distance. The ash in the burn barrel could stop a pistol bullet, but not a bullet from his high powered rifle.

Chandler was trapped.

She had to act now.

She dug around in her satchel until she found Nipper's leash, clipped it to his collar, and wrapped it around a small bush. "Nipper," she whispered. "You need to stay here. And be quiet. No barking."

The dog canted his head and looked at her curiously.

"Down," Amanda said. "Down."

Nipper lowered himself to the ground and put his head on his paws.

"Good boy. I'll be back soon."

Holding the Glock in both hands, Amanda quietly jogged further back into the woods and made a wide circle around the grandson with Chandler's rifle. She kept to the shadows of the woods, stopping at times, listening, careful not to enter his peripheral vision.

A volley of bullets rang out. Amanda ducked, waiting, biding her time.

Walter and his youngest grandson were shooting recklessly at Chandler. Then the report of the sniper rifle pierced the air. Birds scattered from the trees and all became quiet.

During a lull in the shooting, Chandler fired back.

They were toying with Chandler, Amanda was sure of it. If the grandson with the sniper rifle meant to kill Chandler, he already would have.

She closed the distance between her and the grandson in the woods, silently weaving in and out from behind trees.

Fifty yards to go.

Forty.

Twenty-five.

She closed in.

Maybe it was a sixth sense, or just plain old dumb luck, or the twig snapping under Amanda's boot, but whatever the case, Trevor, the grandson with Chandler's gun, turned, spotting Amanda.

In the second it took him to swivel the LaRue in Amanda's direction, she fired off two shots—one to the shoulder, the other nicked his scalp, the force of the bullets knocking him back. Still, he refused to give up. Trevor aimed at Amanda and pulled hard on the trigger.

The shot went high.

Amanda shot again, this time her aim was low. She got him in the leg. Trevor stumbled back into the tree, resting his weight against it. He brought up the rifle and aimed it at Amanda, now running toward him. She sighted the teenager and pulled the trigger on her Glock, emptying it until the slide locked back.

UNKNOWN WORLD

Trevor's bullet-ridden body slumped to the ground, and the LaRue rifle fell to the side. Amanda hurried to him and pried his fingers from the rifle.

* * *

During the distraction, Chandler jumped from his position and ran to Walter while emptying the 1911. The old man dropped like a weight.

Reloading on the run, Chandler finished off the other grandson, who was hiding behind a tractor. The teenager had been no match for Chandler. Coming up to him, Chandler took back his Glock 17.

"It's the man, not the gun," Chandler said while standing over the dead body.

Movement!

Chandler swiveled around.

Amanda stopped in her tracks, her eyes as round as saucers as she looked at the deadly end of the Glock 17.

"Don't shoot!" Amanda said.

"I wasn't planning to," Chandler said. His eyes dropped to his rifle. "Where'd you get that?"

"I took it from the guy who had it."

"He's dead?"

"Yeah. I emptied my Glock into him." She handed his rifle to him.

"That was you in the woods?"

"Yes."

"Anybody else with you?"

"No. Only me, and—" Nipper came bursting through, running full speed, the leash trailing behind him. He came up to Amanda and skidded to a stop. "Only me and Nipper."

"So you got the guy who had my rifle?"

"I told you dynamite comes in small packages."

"Unbelievable. What about the two granddaughters?"

"I got one, Nipper got the other one. You could say he gave me a hand."

"He helped you out?"

"Yes. He brought me a hand."

Chandler looked at her oddly.

"A *real* hand. He must have chewed it off from a dead body and brought it to me. He likes to bring me dead things. I'll tell you the rest of the story later."

Chandler and Amanda kept each other's gaze. A low cloud floated in the sky, darkening the land. Nipper scratched a flea. Cowboy sauntered up to the threesome.

"Well?" Amanda said. She put her hands on her hips.

"Well, what?" Chandler replied.

"Now will you admit I shoot a Glock better than you do?"

"Never," Chandler said. A big smile broke across his face. "Come here." Amanda stepped closer to Chandler and he took her in his arms, hugging her tight. He ran his hands through her hair. "I thought I'd never see you again."

"I'm sorry," she said. "I should have listened to you. I'll never doubt you again."

"It doesn't matter. You're safe. Let's get outta here."

* * *

An hour later, Chandler and Amanda had thoroughly searched the compound and recovered their belongings. They scavenged several additional guns and ammo, which Chandler packed on the mule.

"You can ride the mule," Chandler said. "You're a lot lighter than me."

"Ride the mule?" Amanda exclaimed. "You've got to be kidding. You ride it!" She planted her hands on her hips.

"Pretend you're Shirley MacLaine in *Two Mules for Sister Sara*."

"What? What are you talking about?"

"The movie with Clint Eastwood."

"Never heard of it."

Chandler shook his head in exasperation. "Your generation doesn't appreciate the classics."

"My generation? Last time I did math, you're the same generation that I am."

"Believe me, I feel a lot older."

"Well you're not, so buck up and stop reminiscing."

"Pound for pound, you sure do have a lot of sass in you."

"Then you've got your money's worth. But I'm still not riding the mule. I have my standards. I'll walk."

"Tell you what. We'll ride double on Cowboy. We don't have that much further to go, and Cowboy can handle our weight. If you walk, you'll slow us down. And I'm too tired to walk or to argue with you."

"Sounds like a deal. I'll get Nipper then I'll be ready to go. What about the bodies?" Amanda asked.

"Leave them for the buzzards."

* * *

Great evil had taken place at the Packsaddle Inn, and Amanda and Chandler did not want to leave it intact.

Before they left, Chandler doused the house in flammable liquids, and Amanda had the honor of lighting it.

The inferno could be seen from miles away, and when Amanda and Chandler came to a high hill, they stopped and looked back. The clouds had cleared and orange flames licked the horizon where the Packsaddle Inn had been. The smoke spiraled upwards, disappearing in the darkness.

CHAPTER 15

For a while Chandler had a sense they were being followed. He would randomly check the back trail, and at times he had seen someone on a bike. The person stayed far behind them, intermittently disappearing from view. Chandler shook off his doubts and concentrated on their mission to get to Austin and to deliver Amanda to her great aunt.

It was nearing evening when the man on the bicycle pedaled closer to them.

Amanda was startled at the sudden appearance of the man with shaggy hair, a bedraggled beard, and worn clothes. He had pulled his baseball cap down over his forehead, and she caught him sneaking a peek. He said a quick, "Howdy," then pedaled onwards.

"That was odd," Amanda commented. Her eyes tracked the man as he bicycled faster along the road.

"Yeah, very strange," Chandler said. "He's been following us for a while."

"He was? Why didn't you tell me?"

Chandler ignored the question. "Do you know him?"

"Don't think so. Why?" Amanda asked.

"He looked at you."

"So. A lot of guys look at me. Christopher Chandler, I think you're jealous."

"No I'm not. Especially not of him," Chandler said matter-of-factly.

"Yes you are."

"I've told you I don't lie. If you ask me a question, I'll give you an honest answer. He wasn't looking at you in *that* way."

"Then in what way *was* he looking at me?"

Chandler pulled on Cowboy's reins, stopping him. "I've seen that kind of look when someone is scoping out the goods. It's a predatory look, so for the guy to look at you in that way while I'm here speaks volumes regarding his intention. He wants you. The question is, why?"

* * *

Kurt Durant pedaled the bike as fast as his legs willed it. He had suspected the female rider was Amanda Hardy, but for a while, he had hung back on the road, trying to muster the courage to find out. From a distance, it was obvious Chris Chandler was the male rider. The big man appeared just as large on a horse as he did without one.

An hour earlier, Kurt's path took him past the Packsaddle Inn. Being the scavenger that he was, he stopped to investigate the smoldering ruins. He quickly searched the outer area to check for anything useful. It appeared anything of value had gone up in smoke or whoever had torched the place had already taken their fill. Kurt wasn't exactly squeamish when it came to dead bodies so one by one, he searched the pockets and ripped off the jewelry the woman and the young girls had on. When he came to the old man who was on his back near the tractor, Kurt flinched when the man grabbed his ankle.

"Help me," the man had said. He spoke with difficulty.

Kurt only looked at him.

"Help me," the man said again.

"What's your name?"

"Walter."

"Who did this?" Kurt asked.

"Take me to a doctor and I'll tell you what you want."

Kurt grabbed the old man by the front of his shirt and yanked him up. "You'll tell me now or I'll finish the job."

Walter coughed. "A man by the name of Chandler. Said he lived in Austin."

"Are you sure that was his name?"

"Yes. He was with a girl named Amanda. I've told you what you wanted, now get me to a doctor."

Kurt let go of the man's collar. His head hit the ground with a thud. As Kurt gazed upon the old man, he silently thanked the karma Gods that these people got what they deserved. There had been rumors of an inn near Austin where several people had disappeared over the years, but the authorities would never publically announce the name of the inn. The rumor mill had also indicated the inn was run by an old man and woman, along with their two granddaughters. This place sure was evil, and Kurt wanted nothing more to do with the old man.

"Sorry, old-timer, there's nothing I can do."

* * *

After Kurt caught a glance of the young woman riding double on the horse, he was sure it was Amanda. She didn't exhibit any recognition of him or his voice when he greeted them. He figured the last time she saw him was close to five years ago when he was overweight and sported a close-cropped haircut. If the EMP had done anything, it had caused Kurt to drop about thirty pounds, leaving him with lean muscle instead of fat. With the beard and long hair sticking out of the cap, there was no way she would have recognized him.

Several days prior to when Kurt passed Amanda and Chandler, he had stopped at Holly's ranch under the pretense he was searching for a long-lost relative who he thought lived on the same ranch road as Holly did. Holly had invited him in and fed him, which gave Kurt an opportunity to gather as much information as he could.

He'd lathered on the southern charm, thanking Holly profusely for the meal and fresh water, and complimenting her on how they had successfully dealt with the lack of electricity. To think this was the woman who had a bounty on her, and Kurt had come within a cat's whisker of collecting it. If she had known that, who knows what she would have done to him?

Her home was warm and comfortable, and if it hadn't been for Kurt's allegiance to his big brother, well, he would have stayed a while. When Dillon came in, he took a seat at the table and asked Kurt how the cities were faring, to which Kurt replied, "They're hellholes. Gangs have formed, neighborhoods are cordoned off, people are starving or laying dead in the streets."

Without appearing obvious or too interested in their previous houseguests, Kurt let Holly and Dillon do most of the talking. He learned he had missed Amanda and Chandler by three days. Figuring a horse walked at a steady clip of four mph, Kurt made a mental calculation about how fast he'd need to pedal to catch up with them.

A crude estimation put them about one hundred thirty miles ahead of Kurt. He could pedal a bike at ten miles per hour, so with any luck, he would overtake them before they reached Austin.

While Holly talked, Kurt nodded every so often, all the while thinking how pleased Zack would be.

The plan to deliver Amanda was shaping up nicely.

* * *

Nipper was tucked safely in his carrier, and Amanda and Chandler continued into the night. Weary, wary, they rode without stopping, the mule following behind. They passed farms and dark houses, crossed the winding Colorado River, until finally they were at the outskirts of Austin. Coming to a rise in the land, they stopped and peered at the city.

The streets were quiet, void of the hustle and bustle of morning commuters. A man on a bicycle pedaled along an empty street. A shop owner peered out of his shop, checking the sidewalk in both directions. Using a brick, he propped open the door then went about the mundane task of sweeping the sidewalk.

The east sun was behind Amanda and Chandler, casting long shadows upon the land.

"Do you see the Tower in the distance?" Chandler asked, pointing in a westward direction.

"Yes, why?" Amanda asked.

"We'll be passing right by there. I've always thought of it like a lighthouse, calling people who were lost."

"I've never thought of it that way. I lived in Austin for seventeen years and I never stopped to look at it. I guess I was too young to appreciate it."

"When UT wins a football game, the Tower lights up in orange. You can see it from miles away."

"It's dark now," Amanda said.

"Come on," Chandler said. "We'll be going by it, so we might as well stop and water the horses at the fountain."

"The Littlefield Fountain?"

"Yup?"

"Why there? There won't be any fresh water."

Chandler scanned the countryside. "It's rained here recently. There should be plenty of water in the fountain."

"Why don't we find a creek instead?"

"The creeks around here are too dangerous. Too wooly and dark. Lots of places for people to hide to ambush us. I don't want to take a chance. It'll be safer to water Cowboy and the mule at the fountain." Chandler jerked his head in the direction they need to go. "Come on, we're almost home."

CHAPTER 16

Zack Durant had a restless night in the observation deck of the University of Texas Tower. The wind whipped the twenty-ninth floor during the night, windows rattled, and the cold seeped into the crevices, chilling him to the bone. He woke to the first cold light of morning casting sunbeams on the walls of the Tower.

Shrugging out of the sleeping bag, he briskly rubbed his arms and stamped his feet. It was so damn cold he could see his breath in the room. What he needed was a large steaming hot cup of coffee.

Zack checked his walkie-talkie. He had kept two walkie-talkies and extra batteries in an EMP proof safe in his former car shop. At the time, he didn't know it was EMP proof, but now he was glad he had forked over the extra money at the time.

The walkie-talkie crackled to life. "Bobby, you awake?"

Bobby was Zack's right hand man, and if Zack had asked him to jump, Bobby would have replied "How high?"

"I'm awake now."

"Has Kurt gotten back yet?"

"He just rode in before daybreak. Said he wanted to see you first

thing in the morning."

"Good. Send him up here with a hot cup of coffee."

"On it now, boss."

* * *

Fifteen minutes later Kurt sat down at the table in the observation deck across from Zack, who was staring at him intently.

Kurt poured coffee from a thermos into a mug and set it on the table. His hands shook and a drop of coffee sloshed out. "Here's your coffee."

Zack noticed Kurt's shaking hands, but didn't say anything. He took a sip then set the cup on the table. "It's hot and black. Just like I like it."

Kurt dug around in his pockets searching for a nutrition bar. He took it out and unwrapped it.

"Since you don't have Amanda, I guess you don't have good news."

Kurt nervously took a bite of a chocolate infused nutrition bar, swallowed hard, and said, "I couldn't get her." He held his breath and waited for Zack to hurl a string of obscenities.

Kurt had been given one order, which was to find Amanda and to bring her to Zack.

Failure had not been part of the plan.

Zack, didn't blink, shuffle, or twitch at the revelation, only stared at his little brother. He swung his Barrett M107 to the side then idly twirled the mug, taking a drink. Zack's purposeful movements belied the fact he was seething on the inside, and the vein on the side of his forehead looked like it was about to pop at any moment.

Zack forcefully set the mug on the table, rattling it, which in the claustrophobic quarters echoed off the walls and caused Kurt to flinch. Zack leaned back in his chair, clasped his hands behind his head, and said, "Why not?" The comment was neither accusatory nor inflammatory.

Kurt recounted what had happened when he and Trent tried to kidnap Amanda from her grandpa's house. He told his brother about the bad weather, the first shot that killed Amanda's grandpa, how Trent panicked and decided to try to kidnap Amanda out from under everyone's noses, how the plan went awry, and how he had to leave before he was discovered.

When Kurt dropped the bombshell about Amanda having a new boyfriend, Zack rocketed off the chair. "What! A new boyfriend?" His face contorted into a mixture of rage and disbelief.

A corner of Kurt's mouth curled into a satisfied smirk. Turning the knife a little more, he said, "That's right, and they've gotten real cozy riding double on a horse." With his bravado increasing, Kurt met his brother face to face. "Your luck is about to change."

"How so?"

"Chandler is escorting Amanda to her great aunt's ranch. And you know what that means?"

"Yeah," Zack said. "They'll have to travel through the middle of Austin, past me and my trusty M107 to get there."

After Kurt left, Zack sat back down, thinking. His plan was coming together after all, and Amanda wouldn't even know she would be leading him to what he *really* wanted.

* * *

Since learning from Kurt that Amanda and Chandler were coming this way, Zack had been wound tighter than a rubber band ball.

He estimated Amanda and Chandler were only hours behind him, which would put the unsuspecting travelers near the famous Forty Acres of the University of Texas sometime mid-morning.

Zack had hatched his plan years ago, the seeds of which sprouted while Zack was employed as a grease monkey at a local car dealership. One day he overheard a well-dressed man talking on his cell phone regarding a large tract of prime real estate located on the west side of Austin. He had given directions to the place to his business partner, describing it as five hundred acres, some of it riverfront property that could be divided up and sold into smaller parcels, perhaps one to three acres each. They had talked about a master planned community with shops and cafés, and laughed about how much money they would make. He had said, "It will be like taking candy from a baby."

Zack knew where the land was located having driven the roads the businessman spoke about. Austin was growing west, further into the Hill Country where affluent folks wanted to live, hiking up the land prices—and property taxes—to a level higher than regular folks could afford.

The businessmen had a slight problem.

The woman who owned it had rebuffed all offers to sell, even when the businessmen had dangled several million dollars in front of her. She wasn't married, didn't have any kids, which meant she didn't have anyone to will it to, other than a brother who had moved away from the homestead when he was a teenager. Technically, the brother was still part owner, but at the time, the businessmen concentrated on whittling away the old woman's resolve to keep the land.

Zack had studied the guy, noting how he dressed, the way he talked, even his mannerisms, swearing one day he'd be the one wheeling and dealing. He filed away the conversation, not knowing at the time exactly how it would come into play later on.

Fast forward a couple of years. Zack and Amanda met and began dating. He listened to her blather on and on about her family and a great aunt who still lived on the homestead near west Austin that had been in the family since the mid-1800s.

Zack had no desire to live the pioneer life, but when Amanda described the land and how "no-good" developers were trying to steal the land out from under great aunt, well, he started listening.

The brother of the old woman who lived at the ranch was Amanda's grandfather. So regardless of who died first, Amanda's dad would inherit the land. And since Amanda was an only child, she was sitting on a gold mine. Zack wanted to be part of that.

After the EMP struck, he had commandeered several buildings on the west mall of the University of Texas, making the Tower his headquarters. The Tower's 360 degree view provided Kurt a bird's eye view of the grounds and he'd be able to spot anyone who would try a coordinated attack. If anyone did, it would be foolish. They would suffer numerous casualties.

Zack had at his disposal over twenty armed men who patrolled the boundary of his empire and anyone unlucky enough to accidentally step foot on his kingdom paid a heavy price. Supplies of food and water the wayward travelers carried were payment in exchange for their lives. Most acquiesced to the demands, but occasionally a shot would ring out, signifying the end of a life.

CHRIS PIKE

Guadalupe Street, known as the Drag, signified the western boundary of Zack's kingdom, and was patrolled by his henchmen. Pizza parlors and Chinese restaurants lining the street still contained non-perishable food, and if anyone tried to sneak in to steal any, they ended up with a bullet to the head.

Zack didn't give many people second chances.

He peered out through the windows of the observation deck. The east sun brightened the wintery land, and from the appearance of the clear sky, it was going to be another bitterly cold day.

He opened the door leading to the narrow ledge of the observation deck and stepped out. A waist high concrete railing rimmed the platform. At some point metal rebar had been attached to the concrete railing then bent and attached to the Tower itself, making the walkway safe from jumpers. It also meant it was virtually impenetrable from an attack launched by anyone trying to scale the walls.

Nature called, so Zack took a leak over the railing. Scanning the eastern part of the city, way in the distance he saw riders on a horse. Didn't Kurt tell him Amanda and Chandler were riding a horse? It must be them.

Another thought crossed his mind. While he had never eaten horse meat, he heard others had. Fresh meat would be a luxury about now. Nearly all the campus squirrels had been eaten, and those that still survived learned real quick who was at the top of the food chain, becoming as skittish as their country counterparts.

Zipping up his pants, Zack retrieved a pair of binoculars from inside the building. Stepping outside, he put the eyecups to his eyes, adjusted the focus, then found the horse and riders.

Fools.

He secured his Barrett M107 into place onto the walkway. He retrieved a chair from inside the observation deck and placed it so he had a comfortable spot to sit. His back was against the wall, his rifle pointed in the direction he estimated the horse and riders would travel.

Tonight they'd have a feast and their bellies would be full for a change. The men could use a big meal. Heck, he'd even break out the beer he had stashed in a secret place.

He'd also have Amanda.

103

UNKNOWN WORLD

* * *

Chandler and Amanda rode into east Austin along FM 969, which would soon turn into MLK Boulevard. Coming to the tollway, a plethora of cars, trucks, vans, and eighteen wheelers had been abandoned on the major thoroughfare. When a man wearing a hoodie and low riding pants saw the approaching riders, he ducked behind a truck.

The winding, hilly road took them past an empty jail, an overgrown golf course, looted businesses, apartment complexes, and houses with boards nailed over the windows. Trash overflowed into the street, rats scurrying in and out of the debris, covered by clouds of flies.

"Does the red X mean what I think it means?" Amanda asked. She had noticed several houses with a spray-painted red X on the door.

"It means there's a dead body in there."

"Oh," she said. "Sorta like what happened during the Black Death. Guess we've come full circle in history."

"It's better to leave the corpse in the house than on the street. We've got enough problems without more diseases breeding," Chandler said.

They rode in silence, accompanied by the steady rhythm of two sets of hooves clomping on pavement. People poked their heads out of doorways, intrigued by the sight of the horse and the mule.

When the state cemetery came into view, Chandler said, "Famous Texans are buried there."

"Like who?" Amanda asked.

"Stephen F. Austin for one. He's the father of Texas. He brought three hundred families to Texas in 1825. He was only twenty-four when he did that."

"A few years older than me," Amanda commented.

"His father was the one who worked the deal, getting a grant that would give him permission to bring the families here. His father died soon after, so it was up to the son to carry out his father's wishes. A family of four was allotted 1,280 acres. Farmers less, ranchers more. Most of them settled along the Brazos and Colorado Rivers. It's still prime real estate along those areas, especially the Colorado River."

"How do you know all that?"

"I like to study history and what life was like back then. It was simpler."

"And harder. They didn't have electricity or modern medicine. Travel was by steamboat."

"Or horse," Chandler added.

"Just like what we're doing now."

"Yup, just like now." Chandler paused, thinking. "There are a lot of Texas governors, Texas Rangers, U.S. senators and representatives, Confederate generals, and Revolutionary War veterans buried there. Their wives too."

"It looks so peaceful." Amanda said.

"It is. Haven't you ever walked a cemetery before?"

"Can't say it's on my bucket list of things to do. It's kinda creepy, don't you think?" Amanda looked at the old headstones as Chandler talked.

"Not really. The trees are big, it's quiet. Grounds are manicured."

"It looks like someone is still taking care of the place. The grass has been recently mowed."

"Society hasn't imploded completely yet. Once it does, cemeteries will be the first to go. People will be too busy trying to live to look after the dead."

"Just like us," Amanda said.

"Exactly like us."

They rode along MLK Boulevard, traveling west toward the University of Texas campus. Once they crossed over I-35, Chandler felt more at ease. The big interstate was the eastern boundary of the University of Texas campus and a natural dividing line between opposite cultures of the city. One side prided itself on higher learning, while the other side of the interstate was the killing for a buck side of town.

They were in Longhorn territory now.

"The hard part is over," Chandler said. "The east side of Austin isn't exactly the best place to be. I didn't want to stop anywhere."

The Frank C. Irwin special events center came into view and people stopped what they were doing to watch the riders plod on. They curiously tracked the horse and riders until both were out of view.

Amanda glanced back over her shoulder. "Those people gave

105

me the creeps."

"Be on the lookout for anyone getting too close and don't hesitate to use your Glock. If you need to shoot, remember—kill 'em all, and let God sort 'em out."

They passed the landmarks of the Bob Bullock Museum, Blanton Museum of Art, and when they came to University Avenue, Chandler directed Cowboy to turn right.

"Why are we going into the campus?" Amanda asked.

"The Littlefield Fountain is a couple of blocks away. It will be a good place for us to stop."

The once pristine fountain was choked with litter and covered with green moss. A few people congregated under a tree and looked with awe upon the horse. A woman dipped a jug into the fountain, collecting water. She hurried away at the sight of Amanda and Chandler.

"You think we're okay here?" Amanda asked. She felt too much in the open, too vulnerable, and after the excitement the day before, the last thing she needed was more excitement.

"Yeah, we're okay."

Chandler helped her down from the horse, and once he dismounted, Cowboy and the mule went to the fountain and drank. Amanda let Nipper out of his carrier. He lifted his snout, tasting the air and taking in his surroundings. He padded to the fountain and drank alongside Cowboy.

Amanda sat down on the concrete side. "This had to be gorgeous at one time."

"It was. If you look closely, you can see the inscription," Chandler said. He took a bottle of water from a pack, popped the top, and drank thirstily. "Want some?" he said, offering it to Amanda.

"Thanks." She finished the rest and handed the empty container to Chandler. "What does the inscription say? I don't speak Latin."

"It says 'A short life hath been given by Nature unto man; but the remembrance of a life laid down in a good cause endureth forever.'"

"Interesting," Amanda said. "What cause would you give up your life for so you'd be remembered?"

"I would give my life to keep our country safe." Chandler stepped closer to Amanda and put his foot on the concrete lip, resting his elbow on his leg. "So you'd be safe."

Amanda dropped her gaze. She was quiet for a second then met Chandler's eyes. "Don't die on me. Don't leave me here alone."

"Don't plan to."

Nipper finished lapping water at the fountain. He stepped back and took in his surroundings. He lifted his nose in the air, sniffing the different scents. Some he dismissed as not being important, such as the grackle foraging for food near an oak tree. It was the other scents which disturbed him. Scents of people who he didn't recognize. The air was laced with scents of fear and desperation from a crowd of people he couldn't see. His instincts told him the crowd was dangerous and getting closer. Nipper went to Amanda and nosed her hand, whining. She stroked him between the eyes.

"Your turn now," Chandler said. "What would you give up your life for?"

"I haven't really thought about it. I suppose if I was a mother, I'd protect—"

A mob of people carrying sticks and knives rushed Amanda and Chandler, yelling and waving their weapons.

Cowboy lifted his head from the fountain, his eyes wide. The mule sensed the danger too.

Nipper stood firm and emitted a growl coming from deep within his throat. His ruff bristled along the length of his back.

Chandler drew his Glock and whipped around to face a crowd marching toward him. "Amanda, get behind me!"

A man lobbed a brick and Chandler ducked just in time. The bricked splashed into the fountain.

The faces of desperate men and a few women were haggard, beards unshaven, clothes hanging off their emaciated frames. Chandler had his Glock pointing directly at a man holding a bat. The man made a mock charge.

Chandler yelled, "Stay back!"

"We need food. We're starving," the man with the bat said.

"We don't have any extra food," Chandler said. "We lost our supplies several days ago."

"You've got to have something," the man said, inching closer. "Give us that mule." He nervously glanced at a man standing to the side of him.

"I don't want to shoot you. Stay back."

107

"We haven't had anything to eat in days." The man took another step forward.

"I'll shoot," Chandler said. He swiveled his Glock a fraction to the other man. "You too."

Amanda whispered, "I've got him covered." She had stepped out from behind Chandler.

"You may get some of us, but not all of us," the man said.

"Maybe not, but you'll be first," Chandler said.

Another man slipped away unnoticed from the rest of the crowd and circled behind a building. Coming to the edge of it, he poked his head around the building. Amanda and Chandler had their backs facing him. Brandishing a large hunting knife above his head he rushed them.

Amanda turned, her eyes locked on his. She hesitated, gripped by a paralyzing indecision whether to shoot or not.

The man rushed forward.

Amanda screamed.

Before the man could get within striking distance, the report of a large caliber rifle sounded at the same time the man jerked backwards. The man was dead before he hit the ground, his head blown off.

Shell shocked, Amanda stood there with a strange expression on her face, her mind unable to comprehend what had happened to the man.

Chandler forced her down and they crouched near the cement fountain, taking cover.

The man with the bat bolted to Cowboy. The horse reared up and stamped his front legs.

Another loud crack of a rifle sounded and when the bullet struck the man, he was nearly cut in half.

Cowboy took off running, as did the mule.

A bullet knocked chucks of concrete and brick from a building. Another shot and bark went flying.

The crowd scattered in all directions, some running past Amanda and Chandler, others darting to buildings or behind trees.

"Come on," Chandler said amidst the chaos, "we have to get outta here." When Amanda didn't move, he took her hand and jerked her up. They raced to the side of a building, with Nipper on their heels.

With another rifle crack a man tumbled to the ground, his chest obliterated by the force of the large caliber bullet.

Chandler and Amanda remained still for a few minutes, crouched against a wall of one of the campus buildings. Across the street several people huddled together.

"Amanda," Chandler said urgently, "what happened back there? I told you to shoot if anyone rushed us."

"I…I don't know. I couldn't. There's been so much death." Amanda dropped her chin, letting her gaze go to the ground. "I can't stop thinking about those people at the Packsaddle Inn." She couldn't look Chandler in the eye since she knew she had failed him.

"Those people were evil, and there's no telling how many they've killed. We did society a favor. You have to be tough now, and not go soft on me. It's either them or us, and I prefer us." Chandler got up and peeked around the building. A woman wailed in the distance amidst sporadic gunfire.

"What should we do?" Amanda asked.

"We need to leave," Chandler replied.

"But they're shooting at us."

"No they're not, otherwise we would've been dead by now."

"Was that a sniper shooting at us?"

"Yes, but he wasn't shooting *at* us. He was *protecting* us."

"Protecting us? Why?"

"That," Chandler said, "is the sixty-four thousand dollar question."

CHAPTER 17

Zack cursed his lousy luck. He was sitting on the observation deck of the University of Texas Tower. He had his eye pressed to the scope of his Barrett M107 rifle, swiveling it in minute increments. He searched the circumference of the fountain, checking for any movement near a tree or the corner of a building. He scoped the area and looked for them. Not really *them*, rather, *her*.

"Where are you?" he whispered.

Zack was so focused he didn't feel the cold wind whipping the Tower, or notice his fingers had gone numb. He didn't hear the walkie-talkie crackling.

He sighted Chandler and the LaRue rifle he carried, a firearm of the finest quality, one which Zack wanted to make part of his collection.

Right as he was about to take out Chandler, a homeless guy holding a knife darted out into the open. Amanda had turned around and stood there dumbstruck. Hadn't she learned anything since she had been gone? While she had been in the crosshairs, he had to admit, even thick winter clothes couldn't conceal the memories he had of her.

She still had long, wavy brunette hair he remembered running his fingers through. Fiery eyes that challenged him like no other girlfriend had. Soft skin he remembered touching.

Now someone else was touching her and that made Zack's blood boil.

He couldn't let anything happen to Amanda, which was the reason he had to take out the guy rushing her. Then another one got the bright idea and he had to be taken out too. By then, the group scattered like the cowards they were, even the horse and mule. Zack's shot had been blown and Amanda and Chandler were nowhere in sight.

Now that the damn horse had run off, the bar-b-que Zack had been planning would have to wait. And there was no way he would eat mule meat. He'd have to be starving before he resorted to that.

The door creaked open and Zack spun around.

"What's going on?" Kurt asked. "I heard shooting." He leaned over and put his hands on his thighs. He was out of breath, having climbed twenty-nine flights of stairs. "Generator isn't working. I got up here as fast as I could. I thought you might need help."

"The fun is over."

"Huh?"

"They're gone, Amanda got away."

"How?"

"Let's just say that homeless group that has been hanging around digging through trash needs to go. I was just about to take the shot on that guy riding with Amanda when a homeless guy charged her. I've tolerated them long enough. Enough talk about what happened. I need you to do something."

"Anything. You name it, I'll do it," Kurt said.

"I want you to follow Amanda and see where she's going."

"Sure. Give me your car keys."

"No can do," Zack said. "That car has a bullseye on it. Get your bicycle and follow them."

"You want me to shoot the guy with her?"

"No. I want you to follow them and tell me where she goes. And don't get caught. Hang back far enough to where they won't notice you. It's not like they're in a car and can speed away."

"What are you going to do?"

"Make sure the homeless people don't cause any more trouble."

CHAPTER 18

Amanda and Chandler had made their way back to MLK Boulevard by hugging the perimeters of buildings and using trees as cover. Nipper mirrored their movements and was so close to Amanda's heels he nearly tripped her several times. The wary dog was jumpy and flinched at any sound out of the ordinary.

The last time they saw Cowboy, he had bolted to the cross street they had taken to get to the fountain.

"We need to find Cowboy," Chandler said. He scanned in all directions, looking for the horse. "Otherwise, it's going to be a long walk to my parents' house."

"Where do they live?" Amanda asked.

"About fifteen miles from here. They're in a subdivision west of 2222 and 620. Can you make it that far?"

"After what we've been through, I can make it anywhere."

"Stay close, and with any luck, we'll be there later today. How's your ammo holding up?"

"Good enough, as long as we don't get in another shootout. I think I've burned up some of my nine lives."

"Let's get going. Time's a'wasting."

"Hey, wait a moment," Amanda said. "Aren't we going in the wrong direction?"

"No. We need to stay away from the Tower. I think that's where the shooting was coming from."

"1966 all over again. I read online about the fifty year anniversary of the shooting."

"History repeats itself," Chandler said. "I think the university has improved security for the Tower since Charles Whitman sniped a bunch of people. But with this EMP, all bets are off. Maybe somebody has taken over the Tower and part of the university. That would explain why the homeless people were killed and not us. It's a great lookout point with a 360 degree view of the city. The Tower is nearly impenetrable."

For a few minutes they walked in silence along MLK. The morning sun awakened the land and the people near the university. Vagrants sat with their backs against buildings and looked at Amanda and Chandler with growing suspicion. Others were huddled over a burn barrel, warming their hands. When they came to another side street a block away, Chandler stopped.

"Take Nipper and hide."

Cowboy and the mule had been cornered in a patio area of a building by two men. The big horse had his back to a wall, dwarfing the mule. One of the men held the reins while his companion struggled to mount the horse. He had one foot in a stirrup, both hands on the saddle horn. Cowboy stamped his hooves and tossed his head, trying to throw the man.

"I wouldn't do that if I was you," Chandler said. "The horse is mine."

"Oh, yeah? Prove it," the man said.

Pointing a Glock at the man, Chandler said, "This is all the proof I need, so back off!"

They men exchanged wary looks.

"We didn't mean any harm. Saw us a horse without a rider, thought we'd help it, that's all." The man sidestepped away from Cowboy. He pivoted quickly and brought up a 38 special.

Chandler dropped him with one well-placed round. He swiveled his Glock to the other guy. "You're next, so unless you want a bullet to the head, you'd better get outta here."

The man didn't need to be told twice. Keeping his eyes on Chandler, he hugged the side of the building, and when he came to the corner, he sprinted away, disappearing.

Chandler strolled over to Cowboy and took the reins. The dead man had fallen face up. Chandler nudged him with a boot to make sure he was dead. There was no movement. Satisfied the man was not a danger, Chandler patted Cowboy. "You okay, big boy?" His hands roamed over Cowboy, checking for any injuries. Finding none, he opened the saddlebags, inspecting the contents. They had been lucky. Nothing had been taken. The mule looked to be okay as well, and Chandler tied the rope to Cowboy.

Amanda walked up to the scene holding Nipper by a leash. The dog tugged toward the dead man. Amanda held him back. "Are you okay?"

"I'm okay, but he's not," Chandler said pointing to the dead man.

Amanda looked at the man. "Do you want me to go through his pockets?"

"No. Let's leave. I don't want to run into any more trouble. Like you, I think I've used another one of my nine lives."

* * *

Hours later, the weary travelers came to Austin's Loop 360 Bridge, a through-arch bridge connecting the northern and southern sections of the loop on the west side of Austin. The loop, known as the Capital of Texas Highway, snaked along the limestone hills dotted with cedars and affluent homes. The 1,150 foot long 600 short ton bridge had a 600 foot arch with a weathered rust finish, making it an aesthetically pleasing centerpiece of the loop.

A man in a canoe on the lake cast out a fishing line and kept an eye on the brightly colored fishing bob. He ignored the incoming travelers.

"Be on the lookout," Chandler warned Amanda. "Look for any movement where none should be, especially in the hills or on top of the bridge. This is a perfect spot for an ambush."

"Can't we go another way?"

"We could, but we won't. It would take us days to travel around the lake, and since our food and water are running low, it's not an

115

option. We have to push through. It's the most direct route to my home. I'll keep my eyes on the men patrolling the bridge. Get your gun ready, but keep it hidden. And let me do the talking."

Vintage Ford trucks blocked the entrance to the bridge. Several men dressed in Western attire, complete with slickers and hats, tracked Amanda and Chandler as they came closer. Two were young men, the other twice their age.

Chandler eyed the men, sizing them up, noting their hands and faces had not been weathered from the sun. They looked as if they could have been bankers or part of the dot.com crowd before the grid went down. Currently they looked like they might be extras for a film crew recreating the shootout at Tombstone. Or perhaps they were members of SASS, the Single Action Shooters Society—Sassy, as Chandler liked to call the members.

One of the younger men peered over the rim of his aviator sunglasses, eyeing Chandler and Amanda.

Chandler immediately recognized the firearms. Aviator guy had a Colt single action army revolver, while his sidekick had a more modern Ruger Vaquero known for its sturdy construction and transfer bar safety. It had a 5.5 inch barrel in polished stainless steel. The older of the men held a Model 1873 lever action rifle.

A collector of Western firearms would appreciate their choices.

Chandler figured the older man must be the leader when he spotted Amanda and Chandler first. He handed his binoculars to Aviator guy.

The older guy was on his game. So was Chandler.

"That's far enough," the older man said.

"We don't want trouble," Chandler replied. "I'm only looking to cross."

"You live around here?"

"Yes."

"Got proof?"

"No. I don't have any identification."

"We can't let you in then."

"We've come a long way," Chandler said. "Been shot at, we're cold, tired, and hungry. My parents live about five miles from here, and all we want to do is get home."

One of the younger men inspected Cowboy and the mule. Chandler kept his eyes on the guy.

"Anyone can say they live here," the older man said. "We've had a problem with looters, so aren't letting anyone in."

"I'm not a looter and this lady is cold. She needs to get home and warm up."

The younger guy who had sidled up to Cowboy said, "Nice horse you got here. I noticed the mule has a brand on it." The young man traced the outline of the letters PSI and a squiggly line under the letters. "That's the Packsaddle Inn brand." He put his hand on his gun ready to draw it. "You affiliated with them?"

"Nope. Let's just say they are smokin' hot about now."

The young guy said, "What do you mean by that?"

When Chandler didn't answer, the guy cast a suspicious glance at him. Chandler kept his eyes on the guy. "Wait a minute," the young guy said. "I know who you are." A big smile broke across his face. "You're Chris Chandler!"

With mounting confusion, Chandler looked at the guy, trying to recall where he knew him from. He was late twenties, probably clean-shaven at one time, and had on the same type of attire as the others did, cowboy clothes that could have been worn on a movie set.

"Don't you remember me?"

"I'm sorry...I—"

"We went to high school together. I'm Nick Smith. In tenth grade you flattened Jerry Hicks when he was bullying me. Don't you remember?"

Chandler rubbed the stubble on his chin. "Yeah, I remember now. He had it coming."

"You're damn right," Nick said. "The school refused to do anything with that guy, but you took care of him."

"That I did," Chandler said. "It landed me a three day suspension, but it was worth every minute."

"I don't think I ever thanked you," Nick said.

"No need to."

"Dad," Nick said, "this is the guy I told you about."

The older man came closer. "I'm Ralph Smith. Let me shake your hand. You changed my son's life."

"Ah, Dad, you're embarrassing me." Nick scratched the side of his cheek and glanced away.

"Well, he did change your life. After that no good Jerry Hicks stopped bothering you, your grades went back up, which resulted in you getting into college."

"Dad, that's enough," Nick said. "Come on Chris, or should I say Chandler? You go by your last name, right?"

"I do."

"When you came riding up I thought you looked familiar, I just couldn't place you. You've changed a lot. You look older."

"You'd look older too if you've been through what I've been through."

Nick shifted his weight. "No offense. I didn't mean anything by it."

"None taken."

Nick said, "Your friend can warm up in one of our trucks."

Chandler dismounted Cowboy and helped Amanda down.

"Do you have anything hot to drink?" Amanda asked. "I'm really cold."

"Want some hot coffee?" Nick asked.

"That would be wonderful."

"Black okay?"

"Absolutely."

Nick escorted Amanda to one of the trucks and opened the door for her. She expressed her thanks.

Chandler eyed the rifle Ralph held. "That's a nice rifle you got there. Mind if I take a look at it?"

"Not at all."

Chandler took the Winchester rifle and sighted it on a nearby hill. "It's got a good feel to it. If you don't mind me asking, are y'all part of SASS?"

"You know your acronyms. Not many people know it stands for Single Action Shooters Society."

"You *are* dressed for it."

"Oh, these old duds? Thought it would be appropriate seeing that things have turned the way of the Wild West. There's no law here anymore. We had to make our own law because of looters. We've blocked off all the main highways and we're not letting anyone in. You're one of the exceptions."

"Tell me," Chandler said, "are you using full power handloads in that .45 Long Colt on your belt?"

"You betcha I am. No competition loads while we're patrolling.

We need all the firepower we can get." Ralph paused, thinking. "Where'd y'all come from?"

"East Texas. I got stuck there after the grid went down. Stayed a while helping out friends at their ranch. Amanda needed escorting to Austin, and since my parents and brother are still here, thought it was time I came home. Do you know my parents by any chance? John and Tatiana Chandler? They don't live far from here."

"Their names don't ring a bell," Ralph said shaking his head. "This city has gotten so big, so many folks."

"Thought I'd ask." Chandler patted Cowboy on the neck. "Has there been any trouble here other than looting?"

"We're okay here in the hills. We've got the place pretty much cordoned off. We take turns patrolling the main arteries leading into the neighborhood. 2222 being one of them. Loop 620 too. The river is a natural boundary so we haven't had much problem with boaters trying to sneak into the neighborhood. Neighbors are helping each other. Never seen people come together like that. We've got the river for bathing, and some folks are boiling water from the river to drink. There's even been some block parties, if you can believe that. The margaritas were flowing, let me tell ya."

"After what we've been through on this trip, I could use a good drink."

Ralph looked in both directions, reached inside his coat, and took out a shiny flask. "Me and J.D. have become friendly."

"J.D.?"

"Jack Daniels. Want some?"

An expression of understanding washed across Chandler's face. "Sure." He took a drink from the flask and swallowed, savoring the burn. He wiped his mouth with the back of his hand. "Thanks. It's good." He handed the flask back to Ralph.

"Don't tell my son. This is my private stash."

Chandler laughed and patted Ralph on the shoulder. "Your secret is safe with me. Well, we better get going. I appreciate your help."

"Godspeed to you both. I'll say a prayer for both of you," Ralph said. He stuffed the flask back into his coat pocket.

"I appreciate it. That reminds me of something," Chandler said, pausing. "Faith, family, and firearms."

"Come again?"

"Faith, family, and firearms. It's a motto of a wise man from Louisiana. He helped some friends of mine, and passed the motto along to them."

"I like that." Ralph tried out the new motto. "Faith, family, and firearms. I'll remember that."

"Before you go, if you have any trouble between here and your home, take this." Ralph handed Chandler a business card. "It's sorta like a hall pass. I've signed it and dated it. Everybody knows me, so if you run into anybody who gives you trouble, hand them this."

Chandler took the card and silently read it. *Ralph Smith, President, Oak Hill Bank.* Chandler's first impression had been right. They were bankers. He placed the card in his shirt pocket. "Amanda. Time for us to go."

Sitting atop Cowboy, Chandler grasped Amanda's arm and helped her up. She settled in behind him, her arms around his waist. They headed across the bridge and when they crossed to the other side, Chandler stopped, turned around, and waved. Ralph and his two sons waved back.

CHAPTER 19

Cowboy struggled to climb the steep limestone hills formed during the Paleozoic Era when shallow seas inundated and retreated from land, leaving a rich fossil history among the hills. Millions of years before, faulting occurred in Central Texas when the coastal plains bent downward. The more stable interior remained higher. The soft sediments of the Hill Country eroded away, and the hard Cretaceous limestones and dolomites were exposed, resulting in hills and steep canyons prevalent in today's landscape.

Cowboy's steps were heavy on the concrete road of the Capital of Texas Highway. He breathed hard. The sturdy horse marshaled onward, unyielding to the load he carried. The mule acted as if this was a walk in the park.

Cars of all makes and models had been abandoned on the road. Some had been pushed to the side, others still in the same spot when the EMP hit, causing the engines to die.

Upscale shopping centers set back from the road were void of activity, the shops dark, windows shattered.

Gray clouds grew thick over the evergreen mountain cedars and scrub oaks dotting the rolling hills. Terracotta roofs of expensive homes poked above the stunted trees.

Several buzzards crowded around carrion on the side of the road, pecking at it. The large black birds huddled near the head where the soft flesh of eyes and lips were easily torn away.

Curious at what the scavengers were eating, Amanda glanced at the buzzards. A closer inspection showed a man's corpse being devoured. She gasped and put a hand to her mouth.

A break in the low gray clouds appeared, letting the winter sun peek through, shining bright and clear. Amanda sneezed.

"Cedar pollen," Chandler said. "Can't escape it."

"How much further?" Amanda asked.

"That's the fifth time in two days you've asked me that," Chandler replied.

"Didn't know you were counting."

"Kinda hard not to."

"Well?"

"Well, what?"

Amanda rolled her eyes. "How much further?"

"That makes six times."

"You are exasperating, Christopher Chandler." Amanda knuckle punched him on his arm.

"My mom calls me that, but only when she's mad at me."

"Make that two people who call you that when they're mad at you."

"Okay, okay. I'm only teasing you. We have about thirty more minutes until we're home. Like I said, my parents will love you. My brother too."

"Tell me their names again."

"My brother's name is Luke, my parents are John and Tatiana. My sister's name is Katherine. We call her Kate."

"I didn't know you had a sister," Amanda said.

"I haven't seen her much lately, especially since she was the youngest one, and me being older, well, I was always off doing things, so we never did much together. She and Luke were closer. Man, are they going to be surprised when they see me! I can't wait. Oh, one more thing. I completely forgot to tell you...wait till you meet Uncle Billy."

CHRIS PIKE

* * *

The former Big View Ranch had been established in the 1800s by William and Agnes Chandler, immigrants of English origin. They settled on fertile land near the Colorado River, unknowingly building their one room cabin in the hundred year flood plain. Ten years later a flood washed away the cabin. During those ten years, Agnes had given birth to five children, three of whom had survived. The ranch had prospered and William decided they needed a bigger, grander house, so he commissioned carpenters and an architect to build a two-story house on high ground above the flood line. He marked the line by planting ten pecan trees so future generations would know how far the flood waters had risen.

To this day, seven of those trees still lived and produced a good crop of pecans. The trees created a luxurious canopy in the summer, while a healthy pecan crop could be harvested in the winter.

Fast forward to present day where the only remaining male heir, John Chandler, and his family lived. The ranch had been divided and sold off, and the Chandler family had only been able to keep the old house, along with ten acres, thick with oaks and cedars, animal trails, and dens.

One acre of land near the house had been cleared for an orchard of peach and plum trees, while the other half had been cultivated for planting vegetables.

The house sat at the end of a cul-de-sac, surrounded by million dollar homes with swimming pools and manicured lawns. Speedboats were docked at the individual boat ramps.

The once pristine woodland and ranchland of the Big View Ranch had succumbed to developers and the unmerciful blades of bulldozers making way for a perfect grid of streets and houses. Concrete covered native grasses, old wood oaks and cedars growing for hundreds of years had been chain-sawed down in a matter of minutes.

Such was the way of progress.

William Chandler (named after his great-grandfather), John's brother, was known as Uncle Billy. He was a lifelong bachelor, and always looked out for the other guy. He had a casual demeanor, but after he came back from the war, he was a changed man. He never fully recovered from his wartime duty, nor had he successfully transitioned from military to civilian life. He hopped from job to job, being fired from several after getting into fistfights with his bosses.

He tried to hide his problems with humor and a six pack which was never far from his reach.

The years had softened Uncle Billy into a man whose main pleasure was shucking pecan hulls to pass the time. When the weather was better—and the weather never quite got to his liking—he planned to go fishing. It was always too hot or too windy, too cloudy, too many boaters out on the lake, although he always told the tale about the big one that got away the time he was fishing at Mansfield Damn. Each time he told the story, the catfish magically gained a pound or two, along with growing an inch.

Being the older of the two, John had always felt a responsibility to Billy, telling him, "You're always welcome to live at my house." The tradeoff was mutually beneficial. While John was being transferred around the United States during his military career, Uncle Billy stayed at the Big View home base and helped raise his nephews and niece. He had been babysitter, gardener, handyman, chauffeur, and helped the kids with homework, that was, until they were in sixth grade. Uncle Billy never was much good with math, but he prided himself on teaching his nephews how to shoot.

He understood his place in the family dynamics and never badmouthed or talked smack about his big brother, nor did he try to replace him as a father or to dispense punishment. Uncle Billy considered that the parents' responsibility. The kids weren't bad, just did the things kids do of shucking chores and back talking to their mom. Tatiana did most of the punishing due to John being gone, but as time passed and the kids grew into young adults, it became less of an issue. Whenever John came home, the kids were on their best behavior.

While John was the more successful of the brothers, Billy never held a grudge against him. In fact, he had done the opposite, bragging to anybody within earshot about his great brother and his wonderful family. It never crossed his mind to do otherwise. They were his family and he helped them out, earning his way and place in the family. It's what family did: they helped each other.

On this particular day, the Chandlers were getting ready to host a block party. Luke had bagged a deer the previous day when he had walked along the river, scouting for anything that might be useful.

The hills were thick with oaks and cedars, tangled mustang grape vines, making a wild habit among the urban sprawl. When he came to an area known as Panther Hollow, he stopped and looked over his shoulder.

The tale of how Panther Hollow got its name flashed in his memory. When he was a kid, Uncle Billy had told him the area received its name back in the 1920s due to a local landowner losing several goats to a predator. Sometime after that, a panther had been spotted lurking in the shadows of the woodland. Whenever Uncle Billy told stories, he tended toward the dramatic, leaving out pertinent details, and such was the case with the panther story. While it was a true story according to folklore, Uncle Billy failed to mention it happened in the 1920s, the panther had been killed, and none had been seen since.

Luke had been scared out of his wits as a kid after learning about the panther. That night, he had slept with the light on.

Whenever it was quiet and strange sounds emanated from the woods, Luke paid extra attention and glanced over his shoulder more than necessary. Panthers were like ghosts, or maybe coyotes, although he had seen several coyotes lately, but always from a distance. He had yet to see or hear a panther.

Ahead of him in a bend in the river where civilization had not yet crowded out animal life, he'd spotted the deer. He had been downwind of the deer, and the moment Luke saw it, he froze. The deer lifted its head, swished its tail, then went back to nibbling the tender grass.

Luke felled the deer with one well-placed shot. Unable to drag it back to the house, he covered the deer with tree limbs then sprinted two miles back to the house.

Uncle Billy drove the truck, which dated from the early 1970s, while Luke rode shotgun, and due to the location of the deer, they took the long way around until he came to a dead end. He turned the truck around, hopped the curb, then bounced along the uneven ground until they came to the deer. With Luke's help, they heaved it into the truck bed. Without a smokehouse or other means of preserving the meat, they decided to share it with neighbors. Word spread quickly and each family had been asked to bring a covered dish to the potluck dinner.

By late afternoon, the sun had warmed the temperature to nearly sixty degrees. Luke had shrugged off his jacket, and Uncle Billy had rolled up his sleeves, ready to get his hands dirty.

Tatiana was in the kitchen cutting vegetables and a loaf of bread she had baked earlier over a fire. It wasn't exactly Mrs. Baird's quality, but if anyone complained, she'd tell them to make it themselves next time. Making bread and kneading it on the kitchen counter required elbow grease, and a lot of it. Muscles were mandatory, and whenever someone said cooking wasn't work, she bristled.

Earlier in the afternoon, Tatiana had mixed a batch of spiced tea for the guests who wanted something hot to drink. The old family recipe required one cup of Tang, half a cup of instant tea, one package of instant lemonade, and half a teaspoon each of cinnamon, ginger, and cloves.

She boiled water using the wood burning stove that hadn't been in use since the 1950s. It had taken John a while to clean it out and get it working again, resulting in Tatiana forgoing using it as a display shelf for Christmas elves.

Tatiana measured two heaping teaspoons of the spiced tea mix into each mug. She offered everyone a mug of hot tea, and when Uncle Billy thought nobody was looking, he splashed in a couple ounces of bourbon, making a hot toddy.

Intermittently, Tatiana gazed out the window above the sink which had a good view of the street. If she hadn't known better, it might have been a regular afternoon. One of her neighbors puttered around in the front yard tending to the garden containing winter vegetables. She still hoped she'd see her oldest son walk down the road one day, imagining he'd be looking at the house, and she'd wave to him, like he did as a kid when he got off the bus.

It had been two long months since the EMP struck, and she hadn't heard a word from two of her children. Adult children were still considered children in her book, laughing when she referred to them as "kids".

Her oldest son could take care of himself, especially since he had been armed and had Luke's truck, not that it did him any good. From what she learned the newer cars and trucks were toast after the EMP, so if he made it home, it would be on foot. At least she knew where he had been headed, after coaxing Luke to tell them where he was going. And to think he had planned to ask a girl to marry him.

Tatiana thought that was lovely, and hoped to soon have grandkids she could spoil.

Her daughter Kate was another story altogether. Headstrong with a temperament that matched her long fiery hair, she had struck out on her own after she turned twenty-one. Kate had tested every boundary known to a teenage girl, often butting heads with her parents. It shouldn't come as a surprise, especially considering her heritage. Tatiana's grandmother was one of the few Russian female snipers that had escaped Stalin's rule. The ability to survive had been hardwired into her DNA, so if anyone could survive in this new world, Kate would be at the head of the class.

Last they knew Kate was in San Antonio working as a bartender at the historic Minor Hotel located near the Alamo. Famous people had stayed there, including Teddy Roosevelt, who recruited his Rough Riders cavalry brigade at the same bar where Kate worked.

Tatiana prayed to the Almighty to watch over Kate. She didn't need it, rather it was for anyone unlucky enough to cross Kate. She had grown up with boys, acted like one at times, fought like them, could win just about any shooting contest, was a tomboy at heart, but was never without a boyfriend. The phone rang constantly, and it was mostly love-smitten teenaged boys. What Kate needed was a man, and a strong one.

Tatiana shook her head at the thought of her daughter. Even with all the chaos, she missed her daughter. Maybe someday she'd come back, just like she hoped her oldest would.

John had been busy in the backyard setting out lanterns and getting drinks ready. He estimated thirty people would show up so he had set out thirty plastic cups along with a black Sharpie. He'd instruct people to write their names on the cup to reuse it instead of throwing it away. Being thrifty was a way of life now.

"John," Uncle Billy said, "can you give me a hand with the table?"

"Sure. Where do you want to put it?"

"Let's put it over here under the tree. The lanterns hanging in the tree will provide light when it gets dark. Plus the fire pit is still giving off heat, so it'll help keep everybody warm."

The two brothers worked together to place three picnic tables lengthwise under the largest pecan tree. Next they positioned the benches.

John stepped back to gauge the placement. "What'd ya think? Good enough?"

"Yeah, it's fine," Uncle Billy said. "Once everybody gets here, they'll be milling around talking to each other. What about beer? Think they're cold enough?"

"As cold as they're gonna get," John replied. "If you can do me a favor and go get them, I'd appreciate it. Pull up the rope tied to the boat ramp. You'll see them. The cans have been in the river since this morning. Be sure to wash off any mud. You can put them in the cooler, not that we have any ice, but it's the best I can do."

Tatiana was still in the kitchen doing last minute things. She glanced up and peered out the kitchen window. Their first guests were arriving a little early and in style. A man and a woman were riding double on a horse. Tatiana wasn't exactly sure who in the neighborhood had a horse and wasn't sure why a horse was needed seeing the neighbors were in walking distance of their house. And then she spotted the mule.

She decided to go out and greet them. She wiped her hands on a dishtowel, smoothed her hair, and headed out to the front yard.

CHAPTER 20

Standing in the front yard Tatiana Chandler shaded her eyes from the sun-glare. Out of habit she had donned a wide brimmed hat to protect her fair skin. With her high cheekbones, good skin, and large green eyes, she could easily pass for ten years younger.

She had tried to keep a positive demeanor among all that had happened—from the lack of electricity, food scarcity, and lack of knowledge regarding where two of her children were.

It had been over a year since she had seen her oldest, and was hopping mad when she learned Chandler had come home early from deployment, and instead of paying a visit to his folks, he had left for East Texas to propose to a girlfriend.

Luke had acted quite secretive by not divulging what had happened to his truck, saying only, "A friend is using it for a little while." After much prodding once the grid went down he finally told his mother Chandler had his truck.

A breeze brushed Tatiana's face and wispy hair blew around her eyes. She tucked the errant strands behind an ear and watched the riders come closer. Maybe her eyes were playing tricks on her.

Maybe that wasn't her oldest son.

The biggest and happiest smile spread across her face.

It *was* her oldest!

Tatiana ran to him, tears of relief streaming down her cheeks.

Chandler dismounted Cowboy and gave his mother a big hug.

Tatiana stepped back and put her hands on his shoulders. "Chandler, you're finally home." Tatiana swiped under her eyes. "We've been worried sick about you. Let me see you. Are you okay? You look a little thin."

"Mom, I'm fine. I think everybody has lost some weight. Can't exactly get a Whataburger with fries and a chocolate shake anymore. I'm starving. Got anything to eat?"

"I'll make you something to eat. What would you like?"

"Anything."

"Who's your friend? Is this Crystal?" Tatiana asked.

Amanda shot Chandler a confused look.

Chandler cleared his throat. "No, Mom, this is Amanda."

"Oh. Okay. I uh, I just thought that from what Luke said..." Tatiana's gaze swiveled from Chandler to Amanda.

"I'll explain later."

"Well," Tatiana said. She smoothed down her shirt. "Nice to meet you, Amanda. You're welcome to stay as long as you need to."

"Thank you, ma'am."

"No need to call me ma'am. Makes me feel old. Tatiana is fine."

"Thank you, Tatiana."

"You kids come on in. Chandler, your dad and Uncle Billy are out back. Go on out there. They'll be tickled pink to see you. Luke's in the house. I'll tell him you're here. Take the horse and mule with you, and tell Uncle Billy to clean out the shed for the horse and mule." Tatiana turned her attention to Amanda. "Honey, you come with me. Are you hungry too?"

Amanda looked to Chandler for help. "It's okay. I'll be out back if you need me," he said.

Chandler picked up Nipper from the carrier and set him down on the ground. The dog tentatively inspected the new surroundings then followed Amanda and Tatiana to the house.

"Is that your dog?" Tatiana asked. She put her arm around Amanda, leading her to the house.

"He is. His name is Nipper."

"He's a cute dog."

"Don't let his looks fool you. He's a killer," Amanda said.

"Is that his nickname?" Tatiana asked.

"I'll explain later."

"He must be a sweet dog. Reminds me of the RCA Victor dog."

"Chandler told me—"

"So you call him Chandler too?" Tatiana asked.

"It feels odd to call him by his first name. Why is it that everybody calls him by his last name?"

"Long story. I'll tell you about it someday."

While Tatiana escorted Amanda to the house, Chandler led Cowboy and the mule down the side yard then rounded a corner of the house. He stood there a few seconds waiting for his dad and Uncle Billy to notice him.

Uncle Billy was placing beer in a cooler and counting them out loud. He stood up unexpectedly and scratched his chin. He looked around like he was searching for something. When he saw Chandler, his eyes bulged. "John! Look who's here!"

John was carrying a lantern, mid-step on a ladder when he turned around. It took him a long second for his brain to comprehend. "Chandler, you're back." The stress of wondering what had happened to his son evaporated in the time it took him to look to the Heavens and say, "Thank the good Lord." His voice was a cross between relief and happiness at seeing his oldest son. He stepped off the ladder, set the lantern down, and went over to his son. "It's so good to see you."

"I'm glad to be back, Dad."

"Have you told your mother? She's been worried sick about you."

"She met me in the front yard. First thing she said was that I looked thin."

"We've all had to cinch our belts a notch or two," John said. "We'll fatten you up in no time at all." John looked at the horse. "Is that your horse?"

"Sorta. I borrowed him for the trip here. Cowboy's his name."

"Where'd ya get the mule?"

"Don't ask."

"Didn't know you knew how to ride a horse." John went to Cowboy and patted him.

"I had to learn quickly," Chandler said. "Uncle Billy, Mom said you can clean out the shed for the horse."

Uncle Billy said, "Ah, your mother has been trying to get me to clean that out for months to see if anything useful is in there. Guess I'll do it now."

"It's good to see you, Uncle Billy. I'm in need of a beer. Got one?"

"Need you ask?" Uncle Billy scowled teasingly. He retrieved a can from the cooler, popped the top off, and handled it to Chandler.

Chandler took a long pull, savoring the taste. "That's good. I haven't had a beer in months." Chandler's eyes swept over the backyard. "What's going on around here? Looks like y'all are getting ready for a party."

"Actually we are," Uncle Billy said. "Luke bagged a deer the other day, and since it was too much for us to eat and we don't have any method of storing the meat, we decided to share it."

"Where is Luke?" Chandler asked.

"He's in the house," Uncle Billy said. "I'll go get him in a few minutes after I clean out a space in the shed. You stay here and talk to your dad."

* * *

Tatiana showed Amanda to the kitchen and served her a cup of hot spiced tea. She set out two fun-sized candy bars intended for Halloween trick-or-treaters which never materialized. Tatiana had hidden the stash of candy, doling it out on special occasions or when Uncle Billy or John needed some semblance of normality. A sweet tooth ran in the family.

"Stay here for a second," Tatiana said. "I'll call Luke. He's upstairs changing." Tatiana stepped over to the staircase, picked up a cowbell, and rang it. It was the method she had used to wake up her kids when they were in school, explaining, "It beats yelling."

"What?" Luke yelled.

"We've got company. Come on down."

"Already? I thought the neighbors weren't coming for another hour."

"We're in the kitchen. Come on down."

Luke took the stairs two at a time and when he came to the last one, he jumped off. When he walked into the kitchen, he stood there puzzled. He didn't recognize the young woman sitting at the table. "I'm Luke," he said extending a hand.

"I'm Amanda."

"Nice to meet you. Are you from around here?"

"No. Sorta. Well, I used to be, but I've been living in Hemphill with my grandfather."

"Hemphill?" Luke repeated. "That's where my brother was going when the EMP struck. Wait I don't understand..." Luke looked at his mom, his mind whirling. "Is he here?"

"Yes," Tatiana stated.

"When? Why didn't you tell me?"

"He just got here about five minutes ago. He's out back with your dad and Uncle Billy."

Without another word, Luke shot out of the room. He bolted through the living area and mudroom, threw open the back door, and rushed to his brother. "My God, it's good to see you, but you look like shit."

"Yeah, back at ya."

The brothers laughed.

"I can't believe you're here," Luke said. "How have you been doin?" He peppered his brother with questions without waiting for replies. "I didn't think I'd ever see you again. Mom and Dad have been worried sick."

"I keep hearing that," Chandler said, "Believe me, there were times when I didn't think I'd make it back. I can't tell you how good it feels to be home."

"How'd you get here?" Luke asked. "Did you walk all the way?"

"I borrowed a horse."

"Huh? A horse?"

"Yup, the one in the shed."

Luke explained what had been happening at the homestead. He said the street leading to the neighborhood had been blocked off by neighbors taking turns guarding the intersection. Chandler told him how he ran into Ralph Smith and his sons on the 360 bridge, and when one of his sons recognized him, Ralph gave him a business card, letting him through. "I showed the card to the people guarding the street. I didn't recognize anybody and they didn't know me either. Otherwise, I may have had to shoot my way in."

Luke rattled off more questions especially about Amanda. "I thought you said you were going to propose to Crystal."

"Let's just say Crystal is history."

Luke punched him in the arm. "Didn't waste any time, did you?"

"It's not like that."

"Whatever you say."

"She's been through a lot. She's brave and she saved my life."

"I didn't mean anything by it," Luke said. "She looks like a nice girl."

"She is. Hey, I'm tired, and we've been on the road for over a week."

"No problem," Luke said. "If you need anything, just name it."

"Thanks."

Uncle Billy came sauntering up. "So tell us, why did you travel all the way from East Texas with her if there's nothing going on between you two?"

"I told her grandfather I'd escort her to her great aunt's ranch, and since it's not that far from here, I said I'd get her home."

"Who's her great aunt?" Luke asked.

"Mayme Hardy."

The change in the demeanor of John, Luke, and Uncle Billy was palpable. Uncle Billy was in mid-drink when he heard the name. He swallowed quickly and set down the beer he was drinking which was totally out of character.

Luke's jaw dropped.

John had been sitting at the table listening to his boys talk, marveling at their strong camaraderie and similar dispositions. Both were tall and strong, and John was thinking how lucky he was to have been their dad. When he heard the name Mayme Hardy, he butted into the conversation.

"What'd you say her name was?" John asked.

"Mayme Hardy."

John, Uncle Billy, and Luke exchanged worried expressions.

"Will somebody tell me what's going on?" Chandler demanded.

"She's been murdered," John said.

CHAPTER 21

Kurt pedaled the bike as fast as he could, which wasn't all that fast considering he was climbing a steep hill near the Colorado River. Why anybody would ride a bike for the sole purpose of exercise on these hills befuddled Kurt. He didn't know whether to throw up or pass out. The exertion was killing him.

He had done what his brother had said, and that was to follow Chandler and Amanda to find out where they were going. Fortunately, he had held back far enough so that he hadn't been spotted. A couple of times he almost lost them, and when they came to the 360 Bridge, he was surprised the guards let Amanda and Chandler pass.

Kurt stayed in the shadows of a cedar break and watched them cross the bridge. They turned and waved to the guards. That was a good sign. It meant they were on friendly terms with them.

Kurt pedaled to the bridge.

Holding their guns, Ralph Smith and his sons met Kurt. "That's far enough," Ralph said. "What're ya doing here? And what's your name?"

"I'm Kurt Durant." Outnumbered and outgunned, he would have to think fast on his feet to convince these guys he was harmless. "I'm trying to find some friends."

"Who?" Ralph asked suspiciously.

"The Chandler family. My parents were good friends with them."

"Well don't that beat all," Ralph said. He lowered his rifle. "Chris Chandler just rode this way. You missed him by minutes."

"Chris Chandler?" Kurt repeated. "Here? Just now?" He looked toward the north then to the south as if trying to spot him on the road. "Which way did he go?"

Ralph jerked his head to the north. "That way."

"What was he doing?"

"He said he was trying to get home. One of my boys recognized him, so I gave him a pass."

"Stroke of luck on his part."

"Are you friends with him?" Ralph asked.

"Not really," Kurt said shaking his head. "I mean I know of him, but I'm actually looking for his parents."

"You know John and Tatiana?"

Kurt nearly laughed out loud at how well Ralph had fallen for the ruse. "Not me personally, my parents. They used to be good friends and wanted me to look them up," Kurt lied. "My parents are in poor health and owed John and Tatiana a debt from a long time ago, and would like to repay them while they are still alive."

"Paper money isn't much good anymore," Ralph said.

"It's not paper money I need to give them."

"Then what do you need to give them?"

Kurt placed a hand over his heart and thumped his chest. "It's a message from the heart. You know how old folks are. They get real sentimental when they're close to death."

"Oh," Ralph said. "Sorry to hear your folks are doing poorly."

"It's been tough on the whole family." Kurt cleared his throat and fake sniffled, glancing away.

"Tell you what," Ralph said. "I'm not supposed to let anybody in who doesn't live here, but since you know the Chandler family, here's my business card. I'll sign it for you. You said your name was Kurt Durant?"

"That's me."

Ralph scribbled his name on the card. "You need to give it to the guards at the next corner. Tell them what you told me and they'll let you through."

"I appreciate that," Kurt said. He did a quick calculation regarding how much time had passed and how far Amanda and Chandler could have traveled. Since he didn't exactly know where they were going, he took another chance. "I go up to 2222 and turn left? Sorry, it's been a while since I've been to their house."

Ralph ran a hand across his chin. Nick, his son, the one who Chandler made sure the bully wouldn't bother him anymore, was standing next to him. "Nick, do you know where the Chandler family lives?"

"Yeah, I sure do. Go up to 2222, turn left, go about a mile or so until you come to the second stoplight. Make another left and the road will wind around for a while until you come to a street called Big View. The house is at the end of the street. Can't miss it because it's the oldest house in the neighborhood."

"I remember now. A big, two-story house?" Kurt asked, hoping the 50/50 chance was in his favor.

"Right."

Kurt breathed an internal sigh of relief. "Thank you so much." He mentally patted himself on the back. Lying was getting easier and easier.

"Good luck to you," Ralph said. "It's about a thirty minute bike ride from here."

* * *

Kurt Durant showed the card to the guards at the next intersection. They let him pass and said the same thing nice old Ralph had said about Chris Chandler. "You only missed him by a few minutes."

"Just my luck," Kurt replied.

Since Kurt now knew the exact location of the house, the pressure was off. He thanked the guards, waved goodbye, then leisurely pedaled the rest of the way. When he came to the top of the hill where the main street ended and Big View began, Kurt stopped to take a rest.

The winding, sloping street meandered along the contours of the

UNKNOWN WORLD

Colorado River. Million dollar houses on oversized lots faced the river where docked boats sat silent. A few kids played hopscotch on the sidewalks where a grid had been drawn. A younger child, perhaps around six years old used colored chalk to draw on a driveway next to a Range Rover and BMW sitting idly. Further down the street, a man cut grass using an old reel mower which didn't rely on a motorized engine.

Each house had a mailbox near the street. As Kurt rode along the street, he made a mental note on the mailbox that was personalized with the last name Andrews.

If Kurt hadn't known better, it might have been a normal lazy Sunday afternoon. Wives would be cooking dinner; husbands watching a football game. The neighborhood didn't look any worse for the wear. He'd have to tell Zack they needed to make a supply run here some day.

He decided more intel was needed on Amanda and Chandler. He leaned into his bike, pushed down on the right pedal, and bicycled along the street. When he came to the house, he stopped and pretended to fiddle with the bike chain, all the while his eyes were roaming over the property. It appeared the Chandlers were getting ready for a party, which gave him an idea. Stepping off the bike, he walked it up to the house, kicked down the kickstand, and leaned the bike to the side. He knocked on the door and someone from inside yelled, "Just a moment!"

The door swung open.

It was Amanda.

Kurt stood there with his mouth open. He had not expected Amanda to open the door, and he was sure she'd recognize him.

A beat later Nipper came running up, barking.

Amanda bent over and held Nipper back by the collar. "Sorry about that. He always barks at strangers. Can I help you?" she asked, struggling to hold Nipper while looking up at Kurt at an odd angle.

"I'm not sure I have the right house," Kurt said. He put his hand to his face trying to hide. "I'm looking for the Andrews. Is this their house by any chance?"

"I'm only visiting here," she said, and Kurt let out a breath he had been holding.

Amanda said, "I'll get someone to help you." She struggled with Nipper, who was using all his strength to wiggle away from her

138

CHRIS PIKE

grasp. "I'm sorry, let me put him up. He's stronger than he looks and has been trying to get outside since I got here. I'll get someone else to help you." Amanda awkwardly shut the door.

Amanda yelled for Tatiana to come to the door.

A moment later the door opened. "Hello, I'm Tatiana. You're looking for the Andrews?"

"Yes. Is this the right house?"

"Lots of people make that mistake. I get their mail from time to time, but not anymore."

Kurt looked at her oddly.

"There's no mail delivery."

"Of course."

Tatiana shut the door and stepped onto the porch. "Their house number is similar to ours. They're up the street." She pointed in the direction. "It's the house on the left, the two-story with the bright red door."

"I see it now. Sorry to bother you folks," Kurt said.

"When you see them, tell Faith to come a little early."

Kurt only looked at Tatiana.

"We're having a party tonight," she said. "You're welcome to come too."

"Thank you. I can't—"

Tatiana waved him off. "Of course you can stop by. We have cold beer on the patio. Go ask my husband. He's out back with our two sons and their Uncle Billy."

"I wouldn't want to be a bother."

"No bother. It's a great day and we're getting ready for a celebration."

"What are you celebrating?"

"Originally it was to celebrate my youngest son bagging a deer, but now since my oldest son is back, we're going to celebrate that. We haven't seen him in over a year. And we've got company." Tatiana checked to her right then left. She lowered her voice and said, "He brought home a girl."

"How nice. Well, ma'am, you must have a lot of work to do and I wouldn't want to intrude on your husband and boys."

"Thought I'd ask," Tatiana said. "Maybe we'll see you tonight."

Kurt tipped his cap and said, "On the other hand, maybe I will pop by. Save me a cold beer, will ya?" Taking the handlebars of his bike, he turned it around and walked it along the sidewalk. He stopped at the street, waved and said, "Thanks again."

"You're welcome," Tatiana said.

Kurt biked over to the Andrews' house and leaned his bike at the mailbox. He strolled up the sidewalk, glanced back at where Tatiana had been, and waved in case she was still watching. Satisfied she had gone back into her house, Kurt grabbed his bike and disappeared over the hill. He had to make it back to the Tower before it got dark.

* * *

An hour later, Kurt was back at the University of Texas Tower, reporting what he had learned to his brother.

Zack was sitting at the table in the cramped room. He had taken apart his Glock to clean it. Various cleaning supplies were laid out in an orderly fashion. On the table was a bore brush, powder solvent, an old toothbrush to clean the nooks and crannies, a jag for pushing cleaning patches through the bore, gun oil, and lithium grease.

"You sure they're having a party?" Zack asked. He took a chamber brush and dipped it in the solvent, scrubbing to loosen grime.

"His mom told me herself. She said something about having a bunch of neighbors over for a potluck dinner because her oldest son was back in town. She was happy that—"

Zack put up a hand. "Spare me the details." He set the chamber brush on the table. "How many are there?"

"Don't know. The party hadn't started yet."

"That's not what I mean. How many live at the house?"

"His mom, dad, his brother, and Uncle Billy."

"Hmm," Zack said. "That means they have four armed men. What about the mom?"

"She looked harmless."

"About as harmless as Amanda looked when she shot that man dead at her grandfather's house?"

Kurt didn't reply.

"Don't ever underestimate someone by their size, Kurt. Guns are the big equalizer. A 45 is just as deadly in a woman's hand as a man's." Zack rose from the chair, walked over to a window, and gazed out at the view. He kept his thoughts to himself as he mulled over what he had learned. "Did you see Amanda?"

"Actually, I did," Kurt replied. "She answered the door."

"What!" Zack exclaimed. "You didn't knock on the door, did you?"

"Yeah, I did. So what?"

"That was a stupid thing to do."

"I didn't expect her to answer the door."

"Did she recognize you?"

"Not at all."

"Are you *sure* she didn't recognize you?"

"Absolutely sure. When she came to the door, her dog started barking, trying to get outside. She was struggling with the stupid mutt and never got a good look at me. Besides, the last time she saw me was five years and thirty pounds ago."

"What kind of dog?" Zack asked.

"I don't know. Some kind of mutt," Kurt replied.

"Big or little?"

"Medium sized. The dumb mutt means so much to her that she made a special crate for him and packed him on the horse. All the way from East Texas."

"How do you know that?" Kurt asked.

"Don't you remember? I stopped at Holly's ranch pretending to be looking for a long lost relative. She and Dillon gave me all the details."

"Oh yeah, I remember now," Zack said. "She must really love the dog."

"I suppose so," Kurt said.

Zack gazed upon the campus and beyond to the center of Austin. To the south, the capitol building stood like a sentry overlooking the city. The downtown skyline of hotels and banks loomed in the distance. Rolling hills lined the horizon to the west. A buzzard glided effortlessly on a cold draft.

"What are you thinking about?" Kurt asked.

"Her dog gave me an idea," Zack said. "Round up two men and get my car ready. We're going to put a damper on that party. It's rude they didn't invite us, don't you think?"

CHAPTER 22

"Who'd you say got murdered?" Amanda asked.

Tatiana had asked Amanda to check on the guys and ask them how much longer it would take to set up the backyard. Amanda's footsteps on the winter grass were silent as she approached Chandler, his dad, Luke, and Uncle Billy. They were sitting at a picnic table, engrossed in their conversation and had not noticed her.

Amanda loosely held Nipper by a leash. When she stopped, she tugged the leash, instructing Nipper to sit on his haunches beside her. He looked up at her for further guidance.

The four men exchanged wary glances. Uncle Billy set down the beer he had been drinking.

"Practicing your Ninja skills, I see," Chandler said.

Amanda ignored the attempt at humor since she wasn't quite sure she didn't hear them right in the first place. "Who did you say it was?"

Chandler sighed. "I'm not sure how to tell you this…"

"Tell me what?"

Chandler looked at his dad for confirmation. John nodded for

Chandler to go on. "Your great aunt was murdered."

"Mayme Hardy?" Amanda looked at him with a mixture of disbelief and horror. "I thought that's what you said. Are you sure it was her?"

"I'm sorry," Chandler said. He went over to her and put a hand on her shoulder.

"Come sit down at the table with us. Uncle Billy, can you get Amanda something to drink? A beer maybe?"

"Is she old enough?" Uncle Billy asked.

"Does it matter?"

"Guess not."

"For the record she is old enough."

Amanda sat on the bench, sandwiched between Chandler and Luke. Nipper jumped up on the bench and squeezed in between them. Amanda's hand went to her dog and she stroked him along his back, then up to his ears. Nipper leaned into her, sensing her anxiety.

"Thank you," Amanda said when Uncle Billy handed her a beer. He had already popped the top. She took a sip, made a face, then took another sip. "I don't even like beer," she said.

Amanda sighed deeply. "I don't know how to feel about what happened. I didn't even know her." She hung her head, her eyes focused on the wood grain of the table, mesmerized by the simplicity of the pattern. She traced one of the swirls. "What kind of wood is this?"

When nobody answered her question, Luke asked, "Dad, do you know?"

John shrugged. "I don't know. Maybe cedar." He shot Chandler a confused look.

Amanda nodded. "My grandpa made a picnic table out of redwood. For some reason, it reminded me of him."

To say Chandler was baffled by Amanda's reaction was an understatement. He had expected her to cry at learning her great aunt had been murdered, maybe even get up and run back to the house. But to talk about wood? It was quite strange. Perhaps she wasn't feeling well. He placed a hand on her back. "Amanda, are you okay?"

She handed the beer to Uncle Billy, who didn't waste any time consuming it. "I met her once when I was little, then saw her again at my parent's funeral. After that, I went to live with my grandfather.

You'd think since she was alone and lived near Austin she'd want me to live with her, but she didn't. She never even came to visit us. It's not like I'm sad or anything. It's just that she was the only connection I had left to my parents and grandpa." Amanda raised her eyes to Chandler's dad. "How did it happen?"

"Well," John said. He cleared his throat and shifted his weight. "It happened before the EMP. It was all over the papers. From what I read, she lived by herself on the ranch. She was somewhat of a recluse and didn't have many friends. She had a maid that came out to the house once a week, and it was the maid that found her. She had been shot once in the back of the head."

"That's awful." Amanda scowled. She put her elbows on the table and rested her hands on each side of her cheeks.

John nodded. "It must have been quite a shock for the maid to find her like that, with half her head blown off."

"Dad!" Chandler's voice was scolding. "Details like that aren't needed."

"Sorry."

"Was it a robbery gone bad?" Amanda asked.

"Nothing was taken," John said.

"Was she assaulted?"

"Not according to the paper."

"My grandpa didn't even know about it. Why wasn't he notified?"

"It happened so close to the EMP I guess the authorities didn't have time to contact him." John paused then continued. "According to the paper, several developers were getting ready to take her to court to force her to sell her property by using eminent domain."

"I learned about that in school," Amanda said. "It's some law where the government can confiscate private land for the good of the people."

"They can," John said, "but only if certain legal requirements are met, and only if fair value of the land was paid. I'm not a lawyer, so I can't give you the specifics of the law. According to the paper she owned the land 50/50 with her brother—your grandfather."

Amanda snapped her fingers. "I remember now. She and my grandpa must have talked about it. I heard him on the phone cussing about the government and how no good and crooked they are, and how they were trying to confiscate the family homestead." She paused and took a breath. "Then he got sick, and I didn't hear anything about it anymore. I thought it had been dropped."

John said, "Well, it never was. Now that your grandfather is deceased, and from what Chandler told me, you are the only heir to your grandpa's estate."

Amanda looked confused. "I don't quite understand. I know I'm his only heir. Where is all this going?"

"With your great aunt gone, and since she never had any children, you are the sole owner of five hundred prime acres in West Austin and a large spread in East Texas."

"But I still don't understand," Amanda said. "If the courts were going to force her to sell, why would someone murder her?"

John leaned into her. "That, Amanda, is what we would like to know too."

CHAPTER 23

Using her thumb and middle finger Amanda massaged her temple. "If you'll excuse me, I'm going to go lie down for a little while. I have a headache."

"I'll come with you," Chandler said.

He escorted Amanda to the house. His mother was at the kitchen sink preparing a fruit salad with canned goods she had stocked up on from the local Costco before the grid went down. She immediately sensed the tension between the two.

"Is something wrong?" Tatiana asked.

"Mom," Chandler said, "is there someplace Amanda can lay down? She's not feeling well."

Tatiana wiped her hands on a hand towel, folded it, and put it on the counter. "Use Kate's room." Tatiana put her arm around Amanda. "Can I get you anything, honey?"

"Do you have any Advil?" Amanda asked. "I've got a terrible headache coming on."

Tatiana glanced at Chandler. He shook his head, indicating that whatever motherly questions she had, she was to save the prodding for another time.

"Sure, we've got Advil." Tatiana opened a cabinet door, pushing around various items until she found the bottle. She handed two pills and a glass of water to Amanda. "Wash these down with as much water as you can. You could be dehydrated from the long trip."

"Thanks, Mom," Chandler said. "I'll take her to Kate's room."

"If you need a change of clothes, don't hesitate to wear anything of Kate's. You're about the same size as she is."

"Thank you," Amanda said.

* * *

Five minutes later, Amanda was in Kate's bed. She had changed into an oversized T-shirt and a pair of sweats. The bedroom had a double sized bed made out of dark mahogany with an intricately carved headboard. It looked like something from the 1940s. A matching dresser with a mirror sat against one of the walls. The bench was covered in a floral pattern. The windows in the room had curtains which were pulled back to let light in.

Amanda pulled the sheet and comforter to her chin. Chandler unfolded a quilt and put it down by her feet.

It was quiet in the room, located on the side of the house facing the Colorado River. John's and Uncle Billy's muffled voices carried up to the second story of the house.

"How are you feeling?" Chandler asked.

"Better," Amanda said.

"Can I get you anything?"

"Can you open the window a crack? I need some fresh air."

"Sure, but won't you be too cold?"

Amanda shook her head. "I want to listen to the wind. It reminds me of being at my grandpa's house."

After Chandler cracked the window open, he came back to the bed. He reached behind Amanda's head and fluffed the pillow.

"Thank you. I'll be okay," she said.

Chandler sat on the bed and leaned into Amanda. "We've been around each other for a long while now, and I know when you're not okay. You tend to get quiet, and for a chatterbox like you are, it's out of character."

"I don't know what I'm going to do." Amanda propped herself

up on her elbows and adjusted the pillow behind her back, sat up, and leaned against the pillow. "I don't have any family left. There's nothing left at my grandpa's except for an empty house. I can't go back there, and I certainly don't want to stay at my great aunt's ranch house by myself. Suppose the person who murdered my great aunt comes back for me?"

"You're right. It wouldn't be safe there for you," Chandler said.

"What am I going to do? There's nobody here for me." Amanda fell back on the bed and buried her face in her hands.

"I'm here for you." Rising from the bed, Chandler went to the dresser and pushed around a hairbrush and some of his sister's makeup. He spoke slowly and deliberately. "Amanda, from the moment I saw you I knew you were something special, and I know you felt the same. But..." He trailed off, uncertain exactly what he wanted to say or how much.

Amanda sat up straight and faced him. "But what? Tell me."

"When I caught my best friend in bed with the woman I thought I loved, well, I didn't care if I lived or died. That was one of the reasons I had paired up with those jerks who were patrolling the bridge when I met Holly and Dillon. I was self-destructing. I was mad, embarrassed, and angrier than I had ever been. I swore I'd never be betrayed like that again. It made me want to kill, and I didn't care who."

"But you didn't."

"That's not exactly true. I knew that if I didn't help Holly and Dillon, they'd end up dead or worse. I can size people up pretty quickly and I knew Dillon was a stand-up guy. I shot dead the guys patrolling the bridge."

"I don't understand. You used to be a sniper. You killed people, so why is it bothering you now?"

"I was only doing my job so I never felt bad about it. The targets were trying to kill us."

"Just like those guys at the bridge. They were bad and they would have killed you without a second thought. Chandler, I don't care about them. I care about you, and I want you to know that. If I've been sassy, it's just a brave face I put on so people won't bother me. When you're my size—"

"You're pint-sized."

"Right. When you're small like me, you have to compensate

149

somehow. That's one of the reasons I can shoot. A gun in my hand has the same amount of power that it does in your hand. I'm not afraid to use it."

"You've already shown that," Chandler said. "I admire you."

"Me? Why?"

"You showed strength and perseverance on the ride here. You didn't complain and you always carried your weight. Heck, you even saved my life at the Packsaddle Inn."

"I think we saved each other," Amanda said.

"That we did." Chandler sat down on the bed. He met Amanda's eyes. "There's something I want you to know. I've wanted to say this for a long time." He swallowed. "I—"

The door to the bedroom swung open and Luke appeared. Amanda and Chandler turned to look at him. Luke recognized the unmistakable *not now* look his brother shot at him. "Oh…I…uh…" he stuttered. "I didn't know I was interrupting. I can come back later."

"Do you need something?" Amanda asked.

"I think it can wait. I'll just go."

Chandler said, "You might as well tell us. The moment's over."

"Mom sent me up here to get you. She needs help in the kitchen." Luke reached for the doorknob. "You two go back to whatever you were doing."

"We weren't doing anything," Amanda said. Her voice wavered from annoyance to petulance. "Just go, Chandler. I'm going to change clothes and clean up."

* * *

"Well, that was great timing," Chandler said as he shut the door. He shot his brother an indignant expression.

"Sorry," Luke said. "What were y'all talking about?"

"Stuff."

"What stuff?"

"None of your business."

"You might as well tell me, because if you tell Uncle Billy it'll be front page news by morning."

Chandler silently agreed with his brother. Uncle Billy had a big mouth, but part of that had to do with drinking. "Girl problems,"

Chandler finally said.

"Singular or plural?"

"Plural."

"I've been meaning to ask you about Crystal."

"I found her in bed with Brian," Chandler said with about as much emotion as stepping on a bug.

"No shit? *Brian*? Isn't he the guy that got you the oilfield job and the one that introduced you to Crystal?"

"Yeah. When I asked him to look after Crystal while I was overseas, I guess he took that to heart."

"Better find that out about Crystal now before you were married and had a bunch of kids," Luke said.

"I suppose. It still didn't make me feel any better. I was really messed up after that. I should have come home, but I hung around town trying to figure out what to do with my life. Then all shit broke out when the grid went down. Sorry about your truck."

"No big deal. It wouldn't work anyway, and it's not like the bank can repossess it."

"I guess so."

"Luke paused. "So, how'd you meet up with Amanda?"

"Long story."

"I've got time," Luke said.

Chandler explained how he, Holly, and Dillon were on the way to her ranch when the weather turned bad. They saw a light in a house and decided to stop there to take cover for the storm. "Fortunately the old guy that lived there remembered Holly and her parents. We had only been there a little while when the shooting started. Amanda's grandfather was the first to get hit." Chandler mentioned how Amanda had killed a man who snuck in the back of the house. "I can't figure her out."

"What do you mean?"

"At times she acts all tough and independent, then other times she breaks down crying. I can't figure her out."

"That's women for ya."

"Yeah. Women. Can't live with 'em, can't live without 'em."

"If you want my opinion," Luke said, "she's a keeper."

* * *

UNKNOWN WORLD

Amanda threw off the covers and swung her legs over the bed in frustration, anger, sadness, and just about all the other emotions she was trying to suppress at the moment. She was so mad she didn't notice her headache had gone away.

What in God's name was wrong with Chandler? So he caught his girlfriend with his best friend. Good riddance to her. She didn't deserve a man of his caliber. He was a hard man to figure out, sending Amanda conflicting signals and leaving her hanging when he was close to telling her how he felt. If they were ever going to get together, Chandler would have to do his part. Lord knew she didn't plan on making the first move.

Amanda opened a dresser drawer and searched for something clean to wear. She unfolded various shirts and held them up to her frame. Tatiana was right—his sister was the same size as she was. She caught a glimpse of her reflection in the mirror, horrified at how she looked. Her hair was a tattered mess, her smooth complexion bumpy and red from being in the cold wind. She hadn't even combed out her hair from the bath yesterday.

Scratching at the door interrupted her pity party.

She let Nipper in and he jumped on the bed. He put his snout to the covers, running his nose all along the length of the bed, sniffing it, letting his superior senses alert him to the fact his mistress was feeling sad. The man who had been here left his own scent, one which puzzled Nipper. In the dog world, the man was an alpha male, using both his brawn and intelligence. He had never raised a hand to Amanda, or spoken to her in a rough tone. At times there had been conflict between the two but the disagreements had been resolved amicably, sometimes ending in laughter.

Amanda sat on the bed next to Nipper. He leaned his head into her, trying to comfort her. His ears flopped down on the side of his face and his eyes drooped. Her hand felt warm on his back, and like a tether to her emotions, Nipper felt the full force of her anxiety.

He pawed at her leg, and Amanda responded by scratching him between the eyes. He relaxed and put his head in her lap.

"I don't know what to do," Amanda said, as if Nipper could offer a solution. "I thought Chandler and I were a team, but if three people are in a relationship, it just won't work." Amanda was referring to Crystal, and though she wasn't physically around, she knew Chandler still felt the sting of her betrayal.

"But he said I had grit, and I don't think he'd say that about just anyone. You know what, Nipper?"

Nipper perked up his ears and his eyes sparkled, sensing a change in Amanda's demeanor.

"I'll show him. Come on," Amanda opened the door for her dog and motioned for him to leave the bedroom. "You go on downstairs. I'm going to get ready for the party."

CHAPTER 24

The block party started and the normalcy lulled the usually alert survivors into complacency.

Uncle Billy and John moved the heavy and cumbersome all oak Victrola from the living room to the back patio so the guests could listen to music.

Several 33 rpm records were in the slots under the turntable. Uncle Billy picked up one of the albums and turned the cover over. "Hmm. Want to listen to Bing Crosby?"

"Maybe something more trendy?" John suggested.

"Not unless your kids have old 45s squirreled away in their rooms."

John laughed. "If you mention a 45 to one of the boys, they'll ask how it shoots. I doubt they know it's a speed of a record. There should probably be some big band music in the slots."

"Oh yeah," Uncle Billy said. "Found one." He opened the heavy lid of the Victrola and secured it so it wouldn't slam down and placed the 33 record on the felt covered turntable. For an antique, the green felt was in reasonably good shape. A little moth eaten in places, but he could overlook that blemish and doubted the holes would affect the sound quality. Using the crank on the side, he wound it.

"There. I think that's enough," Uncle Billy said. He carefully set the tonearm holding the needle onto the now spinning record. The sound wasn't exactly stereo quality, but considering there was no electricity or playlists, it was as if they were listening to a live band. "Not too bad," he said tapping his foot to the beat. "Not bad at all."

* * *

As the sun was setting, casting long shadows, neighbors carrying covered dishes arrived in a steady stream to the Chandler household. Some came with lanterns, while others carried flashlights not affected by the EMP.

Each time someone knocked on the door, Nipper skidded across the kitchen tile and bolted to the front door. He sensed the change in atmosphere and the unusual energy being generated. His excited barks could be heard all through the house. Although he didn't understand the meaning of a party, he recognized the gathering as one of camaraderie and fun.

At each knock, Nipper barked a warning until Tatiana came rushing. With a firm hand, she held him by his collar until he stopped barking. Once she invited the visitors in she released her grip, and Nipper followed the neighbors into the kitchen, unable to resist the tantalizing aromas of the food.

As customary, the ladies congregated in the kitchen helping Tatiana with various tasks while the men were in the backyard catching up on the latest news.

John and Uncle Billy grilled over the open fire pit.

Chandler was surrounded by several of his father's friends who were interested in how the rest of the state was faring. He told them what he knew, then relayed the unfortunate incident with the small child used as bait, and their scrape with death at the Packsaddle Inn.

Earlier, Luke had given Chandler a bar of soap, a towel, and told him to jump in the river, commenting, "You smell like a horse. If you want Amanda to snuggle up next to you, you'd better take a bath. Otherwise, she might mistake you for a real horse."

Chandler gave Luke the side eye.

CHRIS PIKE

"I'd give you a razor, but I kinda like the beard. The river's cold, so be quick about it."

"What about my clothes?" Chandler asked. "Think I should I burn them? I've been wearing them for a week."

"Nah, you may need them. You can wash them in the old washing machine Mom found in the shed. It's the one that Granny Chandler used in the Great Depression."

"It still works?" Chandler asked incredulously.

"Can you believe it?"

"Isn't that the one we filled up with water when we were kids and put the baby ducks in?"

"Yeah, that's it," Luke said. "It's funny looking back on it. Mom sure was mad at us."

"She never found out about the turtle, did she?"

"No, and I don't ever plan on telling her."

"So who got it to work?" Chandler asked.

"Uncle Billy cleaned off years of grime, jerry rigged a few parts, and got the wringer to work. That's the good news. The bad news is that Mom is making us take turns washing clothes. She said she wasn't about to clean up after us and haul river water to the tub."

Chandler laughed. "Nothing's changed since I've been gone, has it?"

"Nope. Mom can still be a hard ass. I think it runs on her side of the family."

"She used to call it 'tough love'."

"Don't tell her, but I'm glad her and Dad rode us hard."

"Yeah. She said we'd understand once we got older and had our own kids."

After the record setting quick bath in a shallow part of the river, Chandler changed into a pair of loose fitting Wranglers, a woolen checkered shirt, and a pair of boots he found in his old bedroom then emerged from the house and joined the party outside.

Luke looked on approvingly. "You clean up well."

A group of neighbors huddled around Chandler, hanging on every word as he told them about his travels, especially the incident at the University of Texas campus.

"So someone took a shot at you?" a neighbor asked.

"Yes."

"Why?"

157

"We didn't stick around to find out."

Luke was half listening to the stories he had heard earlier. When the patio door opened and Amanda walked out, he elbowed Chandler and whispered, "Look at that."

* * *

"So, Zack, what's the plan?" Kurt asked.

After Kurt provided the intel to his brother that the object of his desires was staying at the Chandler house, Zack gathered a couple of his goons, fired up his red Chevy, and off they went.

By the time they got to the neighborhood it was dark. They had taken a different route so they didn't have to cross the main bridge. Zack parked his car at a vacant house on the same street as the Chandlers.

"Stay put," he said, "and shoot anyone who tries to steal the car. He cut the engine. "We're gonna kidnap Amanda."

"How?" Kurt asked.

Zack removed a rectangular box from the glove compartment and shoved it at Kurt. "Using this is how."

"A duck caller?" Kurt sat in his seat, dumbfounded.

"Yeah. Gonna use it to lure the dog into the woods," Zack said.

"Right," Kurt said sarcastically. "Ducks don't quack at night."

"Yes they do. They make all sorts of sounds at night."

Kurt turned and looked out the window. He huffed. "Forget to bring the dog biscuits?"

"No. I've got them right here in a baggie." Zack reached under the seat, and shoved a bag full of dog biscuits in Kurt's face. "Once Amanda notices the dog is missing, she'll come looking for him." Zack then reached into his pocket and removed a small vial of liquid.

"What's that?"

"Chloroform."

"For Amanda?"

"Yeah."

"Better be careful with that," Kurt said. "If you don't know what you're doing, you could accidentally kill her."

"I'll try it out on the dog first," Zack shot back. "If the dog dies then I'll know I've used too much."

"What if someone else comes looking for the dog besides

Amanda?"

"That's his problem, not mine."

Ten minutes later Zack and Kurt had snuck unnoticed into the thick woodland adjacent to the Chandler house. They watched the guests milling around the backyard drinking and talking, while others were dancing to a record being played on the Victrola.

* * *

Chandler stopped mid-sentence and tracked Amanda as she strolled over to the group. Walking up to them, the men parted like the Red Sea, watching Amanda sail in.

Her transformation was stunning.

She had on a pair of form-fitting jeans, a stylish jacket over a light-colored blouse, which in the low light didn't matter. When she turned around and picked up Nipper, the last thing on Chandler's mind was the color of the shirt. All he could think of was that she looked good. Really good, in the sense he wanted her all to himself, right now. Maybe not right *here*, but someplace where they could be alone, where the lights were low and where soft music played. Like the secluded cove he had found as a kid where winter grass grew and where a cypress tree had grown tall and heavy with foliage sweeping the ground.

Yeah, he'd like to take Amanda there.

He had been so consumed by the betrayal at the hands of his girlfriend and best friend, well, make that former in both cases, that he had been too blind to see the treasure right by his side the entire trip.

A pair of boots increased her height by three inches. Her hair had been brushed smooth, and when she tossed her head, those long locks swept her shoulders. She looked at Chandler coyly and casually flipped a loose end of a scarf tied around her neck.

Chandler got a whiff of perfume, something expensive and inviting. Something he liked.

They both sensed the tension, and Amanda challenged him with her eyes, made smoky with dark eyeliner, her long lashes darkened with mascara. Her lips were inviting, shiny and full, and everything he had dreamed of. She looked him straight in the eyes and teasingly lifted an eyebrow.

Chandler accepted the challenge. He said, "Hold that thought." A quick step and a pivot later, he asked Luke to get him two wine glasses and to fill it with their dad's secret stash, the one he thought nobody knew about. "We'll be over at one of the tables."

Chandler took her by the elbow, directing her to an empty table situated under the canopy of a pecan tree where crunchy leaves blanketed the ground. Nipper trailed obediently behind, carefully dodging pecans and the sharp edges of the hulls that if he stepped on, pinched the tender pads of his paws. Chandler pulled out a chair and motioned for Amanda to take a seat.

"You look really pretty," Chandler said.

"You don't look too shabby yourself," Amanda replied.

Chandler laughed. "That's what Luke told me. Believe me, I took the world's fastest bath in the river."

Luke came rushing over with two wine glasses in one hand and a bottle of wine in the other. He set the glasses on the table and presented the bottle. With a mischievous voice he said, "It's a fine Massolino Barolo. A full-bodied wine, somewhat tempting and spicy, yet at the same time deliciously floral and sweet. It's a perfect complement to wild game, which is on the menu tonight."

Chandler leaned back in the chair, rolling his eyes.

Luke poured a small amount in Amanda's glass. "Taste it please."

Amanda took a sip. "It's fine."

"Excellent," Luke said. "Anything else I can get you? Perhaps an appetizer for the lady, or maybe you'd—"

"Get lost," Chandler said.

"Fine." Luke pretended to be indignant. "Hey, if you need anything, I'll be over there." He jerked his head toward the patio.

"Thanks," Chandler said. "We're fine for the moment. On second thought, take Nipper and give him something to eat. Is that okay, Amanda?"

"Sure. He can always eat."

Luke whistled for Nipper to follow him. "Come on, boy. I'll get ya something good to eat."

CHAPTER 25

Like a good dog, Nipper followed Luke until an irresistible odor wafting from one of the tables beckoned him. He sat up and begged, and when he heard his name, Nipper pawed at the air until he was handed a treat. Being a quick learner, Nipper went to another table to try his luck and to quell his ever growling stomach. His hunger hadn't been satiated since the beginning of the trip, and the alluring aromas of grilled meat, various pastas, crackers, and something that smelled like cheese drove him crazy. His senses were on overdrive, especially his olfactory ability, so when Zack made the first quacking sound, Nipper didn't hear it.

"Louder," Kurt whispered.

Zack blew harder into the duck caller, and this time the dog noticed. Nipper backed away from the table and pricked his ears, listening.

"That got his attention," Kurt said. "Now quieter."

Zack blew a soft breath into the duck caller.

Nipper cocked his head and apprehensively scanned the dark woods. The sound came again and Nipper's curiosity captured him.

He belly-crawled under the fence and stood on the other side for a few seconds. His nose twitched, taking in the odor of a treat. His nose guided him to a dog biscuit on the ground and he gobbled it.

He heard that strange sound again.

Nipper cocked his ears listening. He lifted his snout and tasted the air. His superior senses alerted him to the fact that two men were close by. One smelled of old sweat and of a long journey along the roads of Texas, a scent Nipper had smelled before, and his mind whirled trying to identify the person. It had been a fleeting odor, but like a person remembering a new sight, this transient smell had remained in the recesses of Nipper's mind.

Zack whispered, "Let's move further back." Hunched over, Zack and Kurt drew further into the darkness. They crouched down and Zack used the duck caller.

One unsure step at a time, Nipper inched closer to the men and to that unknown sound. On the ground, blending into the dry soil and rocks, was another biscuit. He woofed it down.

A few steps later, Nipper came to where the men had been hiding. He nosed the ground, sniffing, and a brief memory flashed in Nipper's mind. The odor was associated with a man on a bicycle who had passed them the previous day. The man had said something to Amanda, a greeting of some sort. The scent trail of the other man was full of testosterone and alcohol, an alpha male, one who commanded respect.

No. Not respect, something more primal.

Fear.

That odd sound came again and Nipper froze.

The men had moved further into the woodland, hiding in the shadows, and though Nipper's eyesight was superior to a human's in the dark, he was unable to locate the men by sight. He let his nose guide him to them.

Unknowing to Nipper, one of the men had circled downwind of him.

The music and laughter from the party became fainter and fainter, and Nipper found himself deep in the woods.

His steps were silent on the sandy trail, and when he found a pile of dog biscuits, hunger overcame caution. He greedily latched onto a biscuit, crunching loudly. He stood over the pile, tail tucked, and tore into another biscuit as if it was a prized kill.

There was that odd sound again, ever so faint, and Nipper raised his eyes, searching. He only heard the whispers of the wind and the beat of a soft song clinging to a breeze. He dug into another dog biscuit, and—

A man threw a burlap sack over Nipper. He yelped and flinched. Strong hands wrapped around him and jerked him off his feet.

He bucked and thrashed, growled and snapped at the musty smelling burlap, but the hold on him was strong and unwavering.

Nipper breathed hard against the scratchy burlap sack, held tightly against his snout. And then a strange odor, one of harsh chemicals, burned his nose.

He tried to jerk away from it, to breathe fresh air.

He kicked his legs and pawed and bit until his muscles became lax; until his legs wouldn't work; until he could no longer fight.

An overwhelming urge to sleep came to Nipper. Still, he fought it, kicking his back legs one last time, but the need to sleep was too great. He closed his eyes and his body went limp.

"Hurry up," Zack said, holding Nipper. Kurt had taken the burlap sack off Nipper and had tied a rope to his collar. He looped the other end of the rope to a tree.

"Now what?" Kurt asked.

"We wait until the dog wakes up. When he does, we'll make him bark. Amanda will come, you'll see."

* * *

Once Amanda and Chandler were alone, he asked, "Where were we?"

Amanda raised her wine glass. "I'd like to make a toast to a new beginning."

Chandler raised his glass and clinked it to hers. Each took a sip. "My turn now." Lifting his glass, he said, "To us and to our new beginning."

"I like that," Amanda said.

"You've made me see things clearly," Chandler said.

"How so?"

Chandler set his wine glass on the table. "When I found out about Crystal's betrayal, I didn't think I'd ever find anyone I could trust again. Then I saw you that first time in the barn and—"

"I almost grabbed a pitchfork when you startled me."

"I'm glad you didn't. When I saw you that first time, I knew you were something special. It took me a long time to know just how special. You saved my life in more ways than one. You saved me from becoming something I didn't want to become." Chandler took her hands in his. "I want you to know something else, and this is hard for me to say." He paused and took another sip of wine. "I want what I'm about to say to be a lifetime of what it means. Amanda, I lo—"

Luke came running up and Chandler gave him a death stare. "Again, Luke?"

"Bad timing again?" Luke asked. There was urgency in his voice. "Sorry about that."

"What do you want?" Chandler said gruffly.

"It's Nipper. He ran off and I can't get him to come to me."

"What?" Amanda said. "You let him run off? I can't lose him."

"I'm sorry," Luke said. "He was right behind me and the next thing I knew he was gone. I can hear him barking, but he won't come to me."

"You're probably scaring him," Amanda said. "He doesn't know you. I'll go get him. Do you have a flashlight I can use?"

"I'll come with you," Chandler said.

Amanda waved him off. "No, that's okay. Sit here and enjoy the wine. I'll be back in a moment. Which way did he go?"

"He ran off into the brush at the edge of the property line," Luke said, handing her a flashlight. "He probably saw a possum and went to chase it. Just follow the barking. He won't shut up."

"I'll be back in a moment," Amanda said.

"I'll be waiting for you," Chandler said.

* * *

"Really, Luke?" Chandler was exasperated at his little brother.

"What? What I'd do?"

"For starters you lost Amanda's dog."

"It wasn't on purpose and he's not that far away. You can hear him barking. The dog just disappeared. He probably found a possum or something."

"Yeah, well, let's hope Amanda finds him, or you'll be on her

164

list and I'm not talking about a Christmas list. Secondly, you have an uncanny ability for bad timing."

Luke scratched the side of his head. "Uh, sorry about that. I figured I'd better tell you now about the dog instead of in the morning when he could be miles from here."

"Don't tell Amanda that in case she doesn't find the dog."

"We'll find the dog," Luke assured him.

The two brothers talked for a bit, reminiscing about their childhood and about how incredibly tedious life was without electricity. Half a bottle of wine later, Uncle Billy came over, as did Chandler and Luke's dad, John. They pulled up two chairs and sat down at the table.

John motioned to the bottle of wine. "Where'd ya get that?"

Chandler and Luke exchanged glances.

"No doubt from your private stash," Uncle Billy said.

"And how'd you know about *that*?" John asked.

"There aren't any secrets around here," Uncle Billy said.

John grunted, turning his attention to his sons. "What are y'all talking about?"

"The fact that Luke has really bad timing."

"That's what your mother used to say." John cracked a smile.

Uncle Billy laughed under his breath. Chandler and Luke exchanged questioning glances until Luke said, "Don't go there, Dad. We don't need to know anything else."

"Where's Amanda?" John asked.

"She went to go look for Nipper," Chandler said. He ran a hand over the stubble on his chin. "Come to think of it, she's been gone a long time. Too long. Shhh, listen." After a few silent heartbeats he said, "I don't hear Nipper barking."

"I don't hear him either," Luke said.

"She shouldn't have been gone this long. Dad, do you think something's wrong?" Chandler asked.

"Probably not, but let's fan out and find them. Luke, you go with Chandler. Me and Uncle Billy will check down by the river. Be back here in twenty minutes."

The ten acres belonging to the Chandler family was a hilly tangled mix of thick cedars and stumpy live oaks, part of the area known as Panther Hollow. The two brothers silently walked the dry creek beds carved out of limestone over eons. The flashlight strobe cast an eerie unnatural light on the land. Luke watched the hard and rocky ground for any sets of glowing eyes. Chandler whistled for Nipper, then stopped to listen. He heard nothing other than the sounds of the night.

"Let's split up," Chandler said. "I'll check the area to the north."

"Okay," Luke said. I'll circle around and go to the back of the property then I'll head on down to the river. I can't imagine she'd go this far."

"Something isn't right," Chandler added. "Be careful."

Intermittently, voices echoed off the canyon walls. At times, the voices were absorbed by the night and the thick canopy as if the woodland had swallowed them into a black hole. Chandler looked behind trees and peered into the opening of a cave. Seeing nothing out of the ordinary, he continued calling Amanda's name, stopping to listen for any unnatural sound. He came to a limestone overhang and shined the flashlight below. Amanda could have lost her footing and fallen, knocking herself unconscious.

Torturous minutes passed.

Sweat beaded his forehead and he wiped it away with the back of his hand.

He found nothing so he decided to head back to the house.

Minutes later he was met by his dad, Uncle Billy, Luke, and three other men at the entrance to the gate. Nipper had been leashed and Luke had his hand looped through the handle. The men looked as if they were attending a funeral.

"You found Nipper?" Chandler's gaze darted to the other three men. "You're the Sassy boys." Chandler pointed at them individually. "You're Ralph, and you're Nick. I met you at the bridge."

"That's right," Ralph said. "This is my other son, Owen."

"What are you doing here? And where's Amanda?"

"Chandler," John said, "there's been trouble. Ralph and his sons drove by the checkpoint at the head of the neighborhood a little while ago. They found the men shot dead."

"Dead? All of them?"

"One of them was still breathing and when Ralph found him, the man told him who did it."

"Who was it? Does this have anything to do with Amanda? Where is she? Is she okay?" Chandler fired off the questions.

"Slow down," John said. "A man by the name of Kurt Durant—"

Chandler interrupted. "Kurt Durant? Wait a moment. Is he related to Zack Durant?"

"Yes, they're brothers."

"Amanda dated Zack in high school," Chandler said.

"This is starting to make sense," John said. "Ralph said Kurt slipped into the neighborhood by giving him a bogus story saying he was looking for our house."

"Our house?" Chandler asked. "Why?"

"He told Ralph a crock of baloney about his parents being on their deathbeds and how they wanted to thank me and Tatiana for something before they died. You had just crossed the bridge. We think he was following you." John paused. "Your mother told me a man came to the house before the party. He said something about being at the wrong house, and that when she invited him to the party, he said he'd be back. We think it was Kurt."

"He was real slick," Ralph said. "I'm sorry, but I fell for it. I told him where you lived."

"It's not your fault," Chandler said. "He told you his real name?"

Ralph confirmed he did.

"What did he look like?"

Ralph gave a rundown on Kurt Durant's general appearance, approximate height and weight, mentioning the beard, big eyes, and a baby face. "He was riding a bike."

"I knew it," Chandler said. "He was the same guy that came riding up behind me and Amanda yesterday. He looked at Amanda in this predator sort of way. This has to do with Amanda, doesn't it?" His question was met with blank stares. "Where is she?"

Uncle Billy dropped his gaze. The Sassy boys looked to John. Luke cleared his throat and glanced away.

"I'm sorry, son," John said. He unfolded a piece of paper. "We found this note clipped to Nipper's collar." John handed Chandler the note written on a torn piece of a yellowed paper.

In scribbled handwriting, it read: *If you want to see Amanda alive again, be at the Tower at noon tomorrow.*

It had been signed by Kurt Durant.

CHAPTER 26

Amanda woke to the strange sensation of being jostled around. She opened her eyes a slit, and the first thing that came into view was the backside of a man. He had on a short jacket which reached just above his belted waistline, revealing a holstered Glock. For an instant she thought about grabbing it, but common sense dictated otherwise.

Her hair flopped around her face and when she moved to brush it away, she discovered her hands had been bound. She determined she was being carried over a man's shoulder.

It was dark and the man leaned forward a bit as he climbed a hill. She flexed her feet in small increments only to learn to her horror her feet were bound, which meant running was out of the question.

Self-preservation guided her to be quiet and not let on she had awakened.

Amanda blinked her eyes into focus and tilted her head to the side to see the legs of another man. Dark shapes of tree trunks came into focus. Clumps of dry grass faded away into the woods. The path they were on was lighter than the rest of the woods. Sand probably.

Pretending to be unconscious, she let her body sway with the man's movements.

"Is she awake yet?"

Amanda closed her eyes, listening, and for a moment she thought she recognized the voice. It had a familiar sound, but in her fogged state, she couldn't be sure she heard it correctly.

A rough hand grabbed her hair and forced her head up.

She sensed a bright light probing her face.

"Not yet."

So there were at least two of them which meant she had a zero chance of escaping. She wouldn't be able to run, her hands were tied, and her mouth had the aftertaste of something bitter.

She remembered now.

She had found Nipper and when she bent over to unleash him, a hand covered her mouth with a wet cloth that smelled of pharmaceuticals. She'd kicked at the man, only for him to lift her up and jerk her off her feet. That was her last memory until now.

Nipper.

If they hurt her dog she'd find a way for them to pay.

The jostling stopped, and the path changed to pavement. Amanda glanced down and saw two more pairs of legs. There were four of them now, so whatever plans she had to escape had just evaporated.

"Put her in the back seat."

A car door opened and someone leaned her into the back seat, gently placing her on the seat. She played possum by closing her eyes and letting her head tilt to the side. She felt the weight of one of the men slide onto the seat. He lifted her legs and put them across his lap. Someone else slid in on the opposite side and raised her head, letting it rest against his leg. Her hair fell across her face.

The driver started the car.

She looked through the space between the seats to see two men in the front. She didn't recognize them, but whoever they were, couldn't be good. She doubted they would help her even if she asked.

The man who had asked earlier if she was awake spoke. "I know you're awake, Amanda, so it's no use pretending anymore."

She recognized that voice. Zack Durant no doubt about it. Twisting her body, she shook the hair out of her face and stared daggers at him.

"You son of a bitch! You did this to me?"

"I didn't think you'd come willingly."

Amanda's feet were resting on Zack's lap, and no telling who cradled her head. For a moment she considered kicking him with a well placed heel, but dammit, someone had removed her boots. Regardless, she lifted her bound feet and shoved them at his face. He whipped his head back and her feet hit the side of the car.

She was so jacked up on adrenaline she didn't even notice. She launched her legs again.

Zack caught her on the second try and he wrapped his arms tight around her legs. Amanda wiggled her body and jounced her hips. "Just stop it," Zack said. "You can kick all you want to but it won't do any good."

"Go to Hell," Amanda said. She put her head back down and glanced up at the man cradling her head. He had long hair and big eyes set on a baby face. "Kurt? Is that you?"

No answer.

Amanda continued looking at him thinking that she had seen him earlier. "That was you on the bike yesterday, wasn't it?"

Still no answer.

The driver accelerated and the car was now on a highway. She wondered where they were going.

It all started to make sense now. Just like Chandler had suspected, they had been followed, and it was Kurt who had looked her over like she was a piece of meat. "What do you want with me?" Amanda asked.

"You'll find out in due time," Zack said. He reached over to Amanda and stroked her hair. She jerked her head away from him.

"Is that any way to treat an old friend?"

CHAPTER 27

Chandler looked up from the note. "What do we know about Zack and Kurt Durant?"

"From what we've heard they took over the UT Tower and the adjacent buildings including the student union right after the EMP," Ralph answered. "People were fooled because at first they seemed like they wanted to help people. They got the generators running with the help of UT scientists, and worked with school administrators and students to gather food from area restaurants and grocery stores. They built up quite a stockpile."

"Quite benevolent of them, wasn't it?" Chandler said, his sarcasm unmistakable.

"Everything looked great until Zack and ten of his buddies herded everyone else into a room at gunpoint," Ralph continued. "In groups of ten they took people out and made them explain why they were indispensable. If they convinced Zack, they got to stay. If not, they were shot or hung as an example."

"How do you know that?"

"I heard it from a girl we found stumbling her way to a friend's house," Luke said. "She had escaped by playing dead after Zack shot her."

"Where is she?" Chandler asked. "I'd like to talk to her. Maybe she can tell us more."

Luke glanced down. "She didn't make it."

Chandler's expression turned to one of determination. "Zack Durant is one bad dude. He's not the kind of guy who will bargain with us. That only leaves us one option."

Uncle Billy added with all seriousness, "One option, but three operators." He used the word operator to refer to a Special Operations type who is trained and qualified to operate in the clandestine realm which is exactly the kind of mission they were about to go on.

He set down the beer he had been nursing.

"What's up with that?" Luke said when he noticed. "You never let beer go to waste."

"Gave it up when the note came. I'm stone cold sober and am now the fighting machine of my misspent youth, or maybe middle age." Uncle Billy rubbed his not inconsequential belly. "No scumbag is going to hurt my nephew's girl if I have anything to say about it. That girl has grit."

Chandler knew deep down that Uncle Billy would be quite an asset. "Thanks, Uncle Billy. We're going to need all the help we can get if we plan on rescuing Amanda."

Uncle Billy could make five hundred yard shots all day long. In his day, everyone shot and long range shooting was expected if you wanted your man card.

"What do we know about what we'll be up against?" Chandler asked. He needed one good plan and a backup plan. Failure to cover all the angles could mean death for all of them, including Amanda.

"There could be as many as two hundred people in the complex," Ralph said, "but we estimate only about thirty or so are armed and willing to do what Zack says. The complex is guarded night and day. My son took a tour of the Tower last year, so I'll let him tell you about it."

Owen took a step forward. "Hey. Nice to meet everybody in case anyone missed it the first time."

"Let's skip the formalities," Chandler said.

"Yeah, right," Owen said. He swallowed once. "The balcony at the top is capped with a wrought iron safety cage to keep tourists from falling off, or from anyone taking a last swan dive. Unfortunately, it would offer some cover when Zack shoots down into the crowd."

"Okay, what else?" Chandler asked.

"The stairwell to the Tower is barred by a series of metal gates. You'll have to deal with twenty-nine floors and an unknown number of Zack's loyal thugs." Owen scratched his chin, searching his mind for more details.

"Don't forget the Barrett .50," Uncle Billy added.

Luke slapped the side of his head. He felt like an idiot. "Then that was the guy who I saw at the range with the Barrett. It sounded like a cannon. He was bragging about all sorts of things including using Hornady 750 grain A-Max match loads. He said it could slice through a car like cardboard and could turn a man into chunks of bloody meat. He also bragged about the mount he had. He's sitting pretty in the Tower with the Barrett. Said he has a military pintle mount so he could easily swing it. Since it's a long range rifle, he would only have it pointing south toward the only real long range threats."

"I've already experienced his marksmanship," Chandler said.

"How so?" Luke asked.

"At the Littlefield Fountain when Amanda and I stopped there. I don't think he was shooting at us. It makes more sense that he was saving us from the crowd. If he had meant to kill us, he would have. There must be some reason he wants Amanda."

"Didn't you say he and Amanda dated?" Luke said.

"Yeah, but that was years ago. It must be something else." Chandler got the group back on track. "Can we take him from the ground?"

Owen shook his head. "We might be able to damage the gun, but we risk hitting the iron safety cage because the wind up there can be fierce. I would be concerned about a gust moving a bullet toward Amanda. And besides, Zack might want to pop Amanda right then. We can't take that chance."

Chandler dropped his head, trying to conceal the rage forcing itself to the surface. "There has to be a way."

Luke put his hand on Chandler's shoulder. "Remember how we used to talk about how we'd take out a sniper at the Tower so that

1966 wouldn't repeat itself again?"

"I remember."

"And how we said a shot to take out a sniper could be made from Dobie Center?"

"We were just kids messing around talking like that. Dobie's gotta be around eight hundred meters away," Chandler said. "I don't have anything that can make that shot."

"I do," Luke said. "I've got a McMillan .338 Lapua. It's the gold standard for bolt actions."

"You have a Lapua? No way. The Luke Chandler I know couldn't save a dime, and that rifle costs as much as a used car. How did you scrape up enough money for it?" Chandler's voice intonation contained more than a bit of doubt.

Luke squared his shoulders. "I'm thriftier now, and besides, I sold my .300 Winchester Magnum a while back. The money I saved plus a little thrown in by Uncle Billy was just enough to buy it."

Chandler was still skeptical. "Is this true, Uncle Billy?"

"It is," Uncle Billy said. "When Luke sets his mind to something now, nothing can stop him."

"What about ammo? It's expensive."

"Not when you handload it for two years," Luke said. "I've been using 250 grain Sierra MatchKings. It's 2,900 feet per second of deadly awesomeness. I can make the shot. I know it."

Chandler's face showed a puzzling combination of anger and enthusiasm. He looked at his dad and Uncle Billy for any indication they were with him.

"We're with you, son," John said. "Uncle Billy is too."

"Damn straight I'm with you," Uncle Billy said. His voice was steadfast and whatever buzz he had earlier was long gone. His mind was as clear as a sunny spring day. "Family first. Always."

"Faith, family, and firearms," Chandler said. "It's something I learned in East Texas."

"I like that," Uncle Billy said. "Faith, family, and firearms. Whoever coined that was a real smart guy."

"It's something a friend of mine told me. Her name is Cassie and she's a real strong girl who survived a plane crash and walked out of a Louisiana swamp. She learned it from one of the locals."

"Amanda is a strong girl," Tatiana chimed in. She had emerged from the house to join the men. "Don't forget that, and don't forget me. I can help too."

"No, Mom," Luke said. "This is no place for you."

Tatiana looped her arm through the brawny arm of her husband. "Do our boys know the true story of why my family came here to America?"

"I never told them. You asked me not to," John said.

Tatiana explained she was the granddaughter of one of the few surviving World War II women snipers. The family had escaped with only their clothes on their backs, a pair of diamond earrings, and a matching locket which belonged to Tatiana's grandmother. Tatiana didn't have to explain where her grandmother had hidden the jewelry. The family fled after the war because Stalin had not completely finished his purge. After finding friends to live with, Tatiana's grandmother found work at a gunsmith shop. When Tatiana was old enough to hold a gun, her grandmother taught her how to shoot like the pros.

"That's where I met your father," Tatiana explained, "at the gunsmith shop. One day when the shop was shorthanded, I was working the front desk to help. Your dad walked into the shop with a 1903 Springfield. He said—"

John interrupted. "I said 'Can you look at my gun?' And you replied—"

"I'll look at anything you want me to." Tatiana cracked a smile. "The rest was history."

"You're still as beautiful as you were the day I met you," John said. "And you can pass for ten years younger."

Luke and Chandler were dumbfounded at the revelation. Chandler said, "Never mind, Mom, about the part about how you met Dad. You never told us about your grandmother being a Russian sniper."

"You never asked. And when I tried to tell you, you were too busy with girls or guns, or running off and joining the military."

The revelation was meaningful to Chandler. He had always wondered if his interest in guns was in his genes or a product of his environment. Now he knew. He felt blessed to find out he descended from a good shooter. Good shooters tended to be people who said what they meant and could be counted on when the going got tough.

He expected the going to get really tough tomorrow.

CHAPTER 28

Nobody had slept during the night.

Tatiana had filled the coffee pot several times, using an old fashioned paper filter and boiled water. Coffee had become a luxury since the grid went down and she had only served it on special occasions. She made breakfast during the wee hours of the morning, around 3 a.m. according to how the stars were positioned in the sky.

Walking into the dining room where the men sat, she served a platter of homemade bread warmed on the grill, venison from the night before, and fig preserves. The men drank their coffee black.

The small army sat around the dining room table discussing plans and counter-plans, and attempts to psychoanalyze Zack and Kurt flew back between the Chandler men and the Sassy guys.

While discussions were ongoing, Chandler constructed the layout of the western part of the university using items he found in the house. A tall vase substituted for the tower, a sugar bowl became the fountain, and broccoli from the garden represented the bushes and trees. Old Lego pieces acted as the good and bad guys, with green being bad, and yellow being good.

Chandler's mother scolded him for wasting the broccoli, to

which Chandler responded silently by popping a stalk in his mouth and eating it.

After much discussion, a plan was finally hatched with all the players having their own part to play. If it went right and the deception worked, they'd be able to save Amanda and rid the world of one extremely dangerous and evil man.

The kitchen table was covered with a variety of guns, including Chandler's LaRue counter-sniper rifle, the guns liberated from the Packsaddle Inn, and guns from the family's collection. From these resources, they would be able to equip themselves for Chandler's risky plan.

"Anybody seen Uncle Billy?" John asked.

"As a matter of fact, look who the cat dragged in," Chandler said.

All eyes went to Uncle Billy, who sashayed in wearing a green and brown Ghillie suit.

Formerly invented by gamekeepers to watch over game in large British estates, the suits had been adopted by the sniper community. Construction of a workable Ghillie suit was required for most snipers to graduate training programs. The best Ghillie suits were comprised of a buff colored base layer—such as burlap—to which random pieces of camouflage or plant material were tied, making the person wearing it virtually invisible in a forest or a field.

"What'd ya think?" Uncle Billy asked. He twirled once then took a bow.

"You won't win any beauty contests," Chandler said.

"Maybe not, but I'm after the crown, and Zack Durant is the crown," Uncle Billy said. He was dead serious. "You got the goods ready, Chandler?"

"I've checked and double checked the magazines for the LaRue and they're ready to go."

Chandler lifted the front part of the Ghillie suit and set it on his uncle's shoulders to reveal a chest rack containing pouches for magazines. One by one, he inserted the magazines into the mag pouches then folded them shut. He flipped the front part of the Ghillie suit down then took his LaRue rifle and put the tactical sling over Uncle Billy's head and under his left arm.

"Don't take too many chances, Uncle Billy. Keep to the plan and everything will work out."

"I like the feel of the rifle." Not to let an opportunity for humor go by, Uncle Billy got in one last dig. "Hey, how about we swap even for rifles after this is over?"

Chandler rolled his eyes, looking at Uncle Billy's beat up 1960s vintage Colt AR-15 Sporter on the table. Dabs of black paint were visible over the assembly boo-boos, and the triangular handguards were scratched, making unwelcome clacking sounds when held in a firm grip. The gun had an annoying opposing screw takedown system instead of the military captive takedown pin, so breaking the gun down into two pieces would take extra time.

"Dream on," Chandler said.

"Nothing ventured, nothing gained," Uncle Billy quipped.

Tatiana walked in. She had been busy preparing for her part of the risky rescue plan. She had on a low-cut light-colored casual dress that fell above the knees, showing off her shapely legs. She had pinned up her long hair into a loose bun, and had tied a frilly apron around her dress to make her look the part she needed to play.

"You're wearing that?" Luke asked. "No, Mom. There's no way Dad is letting you wear that. You might get hurt, or worse." Luke shot a glance at his dad. "Dad! Do something."

"Your mother doesn't need my permission," John said. "You should know by now she's a determined woman."

"But, Dad—"

"The decision is mine," Tatiana said. "And that's final." She put her hands on her hips.

"Don't you think the flower in your hair is a bit much? It might draw attention to what's *in* your hair," John said.

"Not at all," Tatiana said. "I kinda like it." She walked over to where John was sitting and stood behind him, placed her hands on his shoulders, and addressed the room. "We're a team. We're family, we're neighbors, and we need to stick together. Besides, people at the university know me from when I worked there in kitchen services. Remember, I stayed there to help out a few days after the grid went down. Before Zack took over. People know me, and they won't question why I'm there." She leaned down and kissed her husband on the cheek. "Honey, after this is over, please take a bath. You smell like gas, like you've been mowing the lawn."

"If you had been mixing napalm, you'd smell like gas too," John replied.

John had been mixing napalm using ingredients he had in the

garage and kitchen. An old cannon fuse used for fireworks would serve as the delay for his homemade black powder detonator.

"Promise me you'll be careful," Tatiana said.

"I promise."

Tatiana and John excused themselves, telling Uncle Billy they'd meet him in a few minutes.

"I think we're ready to go," Uncle Billy said. "Ralph, you and your sons come with me. Luke, you and Chandler meet us at the truck in five minutes. Aren't you glad I still have that old jalopy?"

"For once your hoarding has come in handy," Luke said.

After everyone had left, Chandler and Luke were still sitting at the dining room table, checking their weapons.

"We'll get Amanda," Luke said. "Don't worry. Remember what Dad always said. Aim small, miss small."

"And when everything else fails, spray and pray."

CHAPTER 29

Luke reached Dobie center, a twenty-seven story private dorm located eight hundred meters south-southwest of the UT Tower.

It had become deserted in the weeks after the EMP struck, which suited Luke's purposes just fine.

He pried open a door, and stepped into the staircase leading to the roof. Shutting the heavy door was like closing a vault. A musty odor permeated the stale air. Too dark for him to safely navigate the stairwell, he took a lightstick from his pocket and ripped open the foil packet. Grabbing both ends, he bent it until it snapped then shook it, letting the motion activate the chemicals.

Twenty-seven flights of stairs later, Luke came to the door leading to the roof. Breathing hard, he waited a moment to catch his breath. He cracked the door open, brought up his McMillan, and sighted the Tower to determine if anyone was watching him.

The unattended Barrett M107 loomed dark against the limestone walls of the Tower. Satisfied he was not being watched, Luke assessed the situation. The HVAC equipment served as the only concealment on the roof, but the huge holes in the sheet metal, no doubt made by the Barrett M107, confirmed the HVAC would not serve as cover. As he predicted, he would have to disable the shooter or the weapon or he would never leave the roof.

Luke shook out a cape-like camouflage sheet, formed a hood over his head and tied the sheet to his shoulders. From a distance, the sheet matched the roof color, allowing Luke to blend into the roof. Taking careful, slow steps, he moved into position, trying not to attract attention to his movements.

He peered out over the campus. The morning sun brushed the tall buildings, and shadows on the land grew shorter, announcing the start of another day.

Luke's thoughts went to his dad. He bowed his head and said a silent prayer to the Almighty to keep his dad safe and to let him proceed undetected, since a man moving a pack filled to the bursting point would undoubtedly attract attention. John had taken the extra ammo and magazines from Luke's pack and added it to his own load. Luke had offered to accompany his dad when he saw how the pack straps bit into his shoulders, but John had told him an unequivocal 'no', insisting they stick to the plan.

* * *

The sun rose higher in the morning sky. A flock of pigeons glided to an adjacent rooftop, then swooped down to the ground, pecking. People stirred in the courtyard, shadowed by the Tower.

John had moved unnoticed, hugging the corners of the university buildings and using concealment wherever he could find it. Ahead of him, he spotted a ratty ball of English ivy that had grown wild and uncut on the south side of a building, the dark leafy vines of the ivy twisted and curled, jutting up in the middle. It formed a mass of tangled foliage upon a decomposing stump, perfect for an animal den or even better, a perfect spot to drop weapons.

John inched closer to the ivy. Checking left and right, he disappeared behind the ivy where he dropped the weapons.

Minutes later, he emerged with a backpack containing explosives slung over his shoulders. Whistling to himself as if he had no worries, he strolled along the side of the Student Union where he spied a gardener's cart with a half-empty sack of mulch along with a bag of fertilizer.

184

It gave him an idea.

John nonchalantly placed his backpack under the flap of the mulch sack then took the fertilizer and set it gently next to the hidden backpack. Pushing the cart along as if he belonged there, John managed to smile pleasantly at anyone passing by.

Ahead of him, he caught a glimpse of Tatiana going into a side door leading to the cooking area. It pained him not to show recognition in any way, or else he risked exposing them both. He pushed the cart toward the generator room, his destination.

The generator room contained several metal vents, but only one solid metal door. It had a standard key lock as well as an external padlock. Due to the carbon monoxide buildup, workers could only stay in the room for a few minutes. Obviously in violation of OSHA regulations, it had been hastily put together after the EMP, and it was unlikely any OSHA inspectors would pay a visit.

John assessed his entry options, pleased to discover that some lazy person had chosen to put the padlock in position without locking it. Although John could have picked the lock with a paperclip, he slid a thin blade between the door and the frame then pulled it towards him.

The latch bolt slid back into the door, popping the door open. Taking his backpack with him, John moved stealthily inside. A closely fit metal screen surrounded the generator's controls and main body. He used a crowbar from the pack to bend back the part of the screen touching the wall behind the generator.

John slid the Napalm-filled jugs and the black powder bomb between the generator and the wall, creating enough containment for explosive damage to occur in addition to setting a fire. He went to the door and cracked it open. The area was quiet. Glancing toward the predetermined window, he noticed Tatiana peering at him. His nod was answered by hers, which meant everyone was now in place.

If the twenty-eight seconds per foot burn rate of his cannon fuse was accurate, the explosion should happen in just short of five minutes. Striking a match, John lit the fuses then exited the generator building, briskly heading to where he had stashed the weapons.

Time for the party to begin.

* * *

Chandler had been waiting unobserved within seeing distance of where Tatiana was located. She looked south, nodding once more. Taking the cue, Chandler, dressed in a maintenance jumpsuit he'd swiped earlier, entered the west door of the Tower building.

Two guards stood halfway down the hall near the elevator entrance. They were both armed with H&K MP-5 submachine guns.

"Who are you and why are you here?" the head guard challenged Chandler. "Put down the toolbox so we can search you." The other guard patted Chandler down, checking the obvious places of his waist, ankles, legs, and underarms.

"Nothing here," the guard said.

The head guard tapped the name tag on Chandler's uniform. "Mark Whitmore, huh?"

"Actually, I'm his brother. He's sick and I'm filling in."

Chandler handed over the driver's license he had found in one of the pockets. Fortunately for Chandler the photographer at the DPS had obviously failed photography school. The picture was so bad it could cover half the male population. The guard squinted at the picture then handed the ID back to him, eying him suspiciously. "Why are you here?"

"To check on a possible gas leak upstairs," Chandler said.

While Chandler was being grilled, the other guard checked the contents of the toolbox. "What the hell is this brown crap?" he asked, drawing back his hand.

"Probably sewage. I was working on a sewage backup earlier this morning. Maybe I got some back splatter in the tool box."

"That's sick," the guard said. He made a face and wiped his hands on his pants.

The main guard said, "Okay, let's go on up. The elevators are to your left. Just don't touch anything."

"Whatever you say," Chandler said.

As of now the plan was going as anticipated, but as with a stack of dominoes, if one fell, the others would fall, bringing everything down. Currently, one domino was poised to fall. Chandler thought quickly, trying to come up with a diversion. When one of the guards reached to press the call button, the door to the building opened.

"Wait a minute," one of the guards said. "Someone else is coming."

CHRIS PIKE

Chandler breathed a sigh of relief. The domino wouldn't fall after all.

* * *

Right on time, Tatiana entered the cavernous first floor of the Tower pushing a food cart. It clattered and echoed along the light-colored marble floors which had been recently mopped. Two wooden benches sat on each side. The ceiling must have been fifteen feet high. Ahead of her were two grand staircases and two more wooden benches with curved backs. Across from the staircases were two elevators powered by a generator. Ambient light filtered into the long hallway from doors on each end.

The food cart contained several items to choose from, including energy bars, several boxes of cookies, along with potato chips, Cheetos, Fritos, and canned soft drinks.

"Snack delivery for Mr. Durant," Tatiana announced. Despite being in her 50s, she still had the figure any thirty year old would be jealous of, and only a hint of gray in her thick red hair. She was still wearing her light colored, low cut dress which showed ample cleavage. She had dressed provocatively on purpose in order to distract the guards.

"I haven't seen you before," the guard said.

"I'm new," Tatiana said. She smiled teasingly and batted her eyelashes.

"I got this," the guard said. "Take what's-his-name on up to Mr. Durant. You don't want to be late. And take the food cart too!"

"You get all the fun," the head guard grumbled. He took the food cart then pressed the call button and told Chandler to go on in.

Once the elevator doors closed, the guard asked, "What did you say your name was?"

"Tatiana."

"Russian, huh?"

"You're a smart man. I like smart men."

"Oh yeah?" the guard said. He ran a hand over his chin and stepped closer to Tatiana. "Maybe you and me can get together later."

"Later?" She huffed. "I'm an impatient woman. How about *now* instead of later?" She seductively teased him with her green eyes

187

and inviting smile.

The guard gave her a look that sent chills through Tatiana, although she showed no emotion. She twirled once and tossed a smile to the guard. "Got a closet or someplace we can be alone?"

Without missing a beat, the guard said, "I know the perfect office. It even has a sofa."

"Leather?"

"Uh huh."

"Time's a'wasting."

The invitation had been too tempting for the guard to resist. Taking her by the elbow, he escorted Tatiana to the empty office.

When the door shut, Tatiana positioned herself so she could face the guard. The guard set his MP-5 to the side then cracked an evil grin.

Her green eyes and inviting smile encouraged him to come closer to her.

He lunged for her.

She slapped him and sent him backwards.

"What kind of game are you playing?" he said roughly.

"I have a surprise for you."

"Huh? You said you were an impatient woman."

"I am. Let me take my hair down first."

Both of Tatiana's hands went to the back of her head where she pretended to fiddle with her hair to let it down. She licked her lips and dropped her gaze to his lips. Taking the cue, he stepped closer to her. In one deft movement Tatiana snatched the four inch knife from her hair and thrust it upwards into his throat, twisting it into his lower brain. The guard's eyes bulged and he stumbled back, hitting a wall. He tried to say something, but only uttered gurgling sounds.

Seconds passed and the guard slumped to the floor.

Tatiana went to him and checked for a pulse. Satisfied he was dead, she withdrew the knife from his throat, then cleaned the blood from the knife using the guard's shirt. She positioned the knife back into her hair, fluffed the bun a couple of times, and clipped the flower into place to cover the knife handle.

She had no time to regret her action. He was an evil man, one who needed to be deleted from the gene pool. Using all her might, she grabbed him by the boots and dragged him behind a sofa. Thrifty as always, Tatiana took his MP-5 and the extra magazines. Before she left, she checked herself in a mirror. Her lipstick was still in place and she didn't have a drop of blood on her. She hadn't even broken out into a sweat.

She closed the door behind her and went to the elevators. One of the elevators had not gone all the way to the top, and this worried her since it would be the one Chandler had taken.

* * *

Chandler was a cool cat, one who kept his emotions to himself, so he knew what signs to look for indicating nervousness. Perhaps a bead of sweat on a forehead during a cool day or the twitching of a leg not accompanying the beat of music, and the guy standing to the side of Chandler in the elevator had been twitching without the benefit of elevator music.

Domino theory.

The elevator continued to climb.

Each time the elevator passed a floor, it dinged. Two, three, four dings, and right before the number fourteen appeared at the top of the elevator, the guard pressed floor fourteen.

Domino theory.

The elevator doors opened. The guard said, "Get out. We'll leave the toolbox and cart on the floor."

Chandler stepped out onto the floor. An empty desk sat to the side. It contained an unusable black phone, a rolodex, loose pens and pencils, post-it notes, a tape dispenser, and a note pad. It was quite neat. Behind that were stacks of musty-smelling books. Rows and rows of the confounded things.

The fuse on the bomb in the generator room must be reaching its end, and he could not afford to be stuck in an elevator when the shit hit the fan. The rest of the trip would be in the stairwell.

That made two teetering dominoes to contend with.

The guard had placed the toolbox on the food cart, and had pushed both out of the elevator and onto the floor. He held the MP-5 in his other hand.

"Whitman never mentioned he had a brother. You just walk your ass over there."

Chandler remained silent.

"Why'd you use his ID if you're his brother?"

The selector on the MP-5 was in the full auto position; the guard meant business.

Chandler didn't reply.

"That's what I thought."

The guard emptied the contents of the toolbox onto the floor, scattering a plethora of dirty tools. The bottom of the box had crude, unpainted welds. The guard cocked his head and looked at it suspiciously. Taking a screwdriver, he worked to pop the welds.

While the guard had been busy with the toolbox, he didn't notice Chandler slip his hands inside his pants toward his crotch where, fortunately, he had not been searched. Taped to his left thigh was a small suppressor, while a Walther P22 had been taped to the right thigh.

Once the AAC suppressor was in place, Chandler said, "Hey."

The guard glanced up and received three 22 subsonic rounds to the forehead. The look of surprise on his face was comical. He slumped to the floor.

The sound of the explosion in the generator room rattled the building, and Chandler wobbled on unsteady legs.

A few books fell off the racks and tumbled to the floor. The pens and pencils on the desk rolled off and scattered about on the wood floor, and when the sound subsided Chandler thanked his lucky stars he was not in the elevator.

The lights flashed off, and surprisingly, battery operated emergency lights flickered on automatically. The University of Texas scientists had been thorough in their restoration of power to the complex.

Chandler's uniform was getting hot, and the need for subterfuge was now gone, so he ditched it. He put on the guard's combat vest and looked down at the six spare thirty-round magazines secured by Velcro flaps. He slung the MP-5 over his shoulder and placed it at instant ready.

Chandler popped the last of the weld beads on the tool box to reveal two holstered Glocks and two double magazine pouches. He put one Glock and a pouch on his belt, saving the second Glock and pouch for Amanda.

The food cart was covered with snacks, but the storage compartment was Chandler's focus. Behind soft drink cans and fake napkin boxes were a medium sized backpack and a yellow crowbar strong enough to pop open a steel door.

Chandler breezed past the now useless elevator. Even if it was working, taking it would not be worth the risk. He came to the stairwell, opened the door, and peered in. If Luke's memory of his last tower tour was right, there would be a metal screen door to overcome on the stairway.

Chandler crept slowly up the stairway, his footfalls silent and catlike on the concrete steps.

The sounds of sporadic rifle fire crept down to his position in the darkened stairwell and he wondered how Uncle Billy was doing with his assignment.

Finally he came to the last step. Standing on the landing, he waited for the loud tap, tap, tap of gunfire volleys to conceal what he needed to do. Using the noise as cover, he worked quickly with the yellow crowbar to pry open the metal door. When the firing ceased he took a breather, and when the bullets flew, Chandler concentrated on keeping his work as quiet as possible.

CHAPTER 30

Uncle Billy had crawled along the hard ground inch by agonizing inch until he reached the Littlefield Fountain. His camouflaged Ghillie suit had served him well, allowing him to blend into the winter colors of the campus. From a distance he appeared to be a heap of raked leaves or even a mound of garbage.

The fountain was a monument to University of Texas students and alumni who had died in World War I. Set in a granite pool backed by a thick limestone wall, it consisted of military, nautical, and mythical symbols. The bronze victorious winged Goddess Columbia held a torch representing the Flame of Freedom. She was flanked by an Army soldier holding a large sword, while on the other side a Navy seaman held an oar.

Three hippocamps, mythical creatures that were part fish and part horse with webbed hooves, were sculpted with two mermen riders possibly representing man's discipline, while the middle hippocamp appeared to be driving through surf at the front of a ship.

Regardless of the interpretation or the beauty of the fountain, Uncle Billy considered it to be protection against the Barrett M107 in the hands of Zack Durant.

Uncle Billy stayed hidden until the generator explosion rocked the campus. Taking this as he signal to make his move, he took a big breath, stood upright, and walked right behind the statue of Columbia.

Lives depended on what he was about to do.

He defiantly held Chandler's LaRue OBR high over his head, pumping it in the air toward the Tower which he was in a direct line of sight. The only thing missing was him shouting, "Wolverines!" Instead he shouted, "Faith! Family! Firearms!"

Uncle Billy kept his eyes on the Tower. There, just below the clock, he saw the Barrett M107 swivel in his direction. The large black gun stood out among the sandy colored limestone.

* * *

Zack had been using his Barrett M107, peering through the sights, checking the campus for intruders he hoped had been lured by the note. He swiveled the heavy gun on the pintle mount forward and back, left and right. Without the pintle mount to take the weight, the Barrett's 30 pound heft would soon exhaust the strongest of men.

He expected Chandler to show up early, and he laughed at the man in the Ghillie suit who thought he was hidden. He thought about taking a shot, which would easily obliterate the man, but he held back. Maybe it was a trap.

Zack peered through the sights on his Barrett M107 which he had placed on the walkway of the Tower's observation deck. He watched with humor as the man in the Ghillie suit walked in front of the fountain and thrust a rifle high overhead. Zack squinted at the rifle. It was a LaRue.

His grin turned into a deadly serious expression.

Zack immediately recognized the gun as belonging to Chandler. Only the previous day Chandler and Amanda had been in the crosshairs of his Barrett. He should have taken the shot right then, but had decided against it. He couldn't afford for Amanda to become collateral damage.

He glanced back at Amanda. She sat quietly on a chair, staring straight ahead, and had refused any type of hospitality. What he really wanted to do was to ask her what she was thinking about, but the last time he asked, she told him to go to Hell.

Plan A to reunite with Amanda obviously wouldn't work out, and since a Plan B was always needed in situations like these, well, Plan B was shaping up nicely.

She had finally calmed down after Zack assured her he wasn't going to hurt her, but only if she did as he said, and screaming was something she had been told not to do. Not that she took orders, but a few slaps to the face convinced her to shut up.

Not one to take chances, Zack had zip tied her wrists. She still had on her jeans and jacket from the night before, along with her high-heeled boots she had asked for.

Zack thought he must have interrupted whatever plans she had with Chandler.

Too bad.

She shivered in the bleak quarters of the observation tower, and whenever Zack opened the door to step out onto the walkway, a gust of frigid air blew through. Earlier, he offered her a blanket, but she had kicked it off when he handed it to her.

She could stay cold.

Zack grabbed Amanda by the arm, jerked her out of the chair, and roughly shoved her over to the wrought iron safety grate.

"See that?" he said.

Amanda looked out over the campus. "What?" she replied tersely. "I don't see anything."

Zack squeezed her chin and forced her face in the direction of the fountain. "Now do you see it?"

Amanda's gaze went to the fountain. She squinted at the figure in the Ghillie suit thrusting a rifle in the air. "Yeah, I see it. So what?"

"That's your boyfriend who's come to rescue you."

"What? No," Amanda pleaded. "Don't hurt him. I'll do whatever you want me to do. Just don't hurt him. What is it that you want?"

"The five hundred acres you inherited."

"What?"

"Your great aunt's estate. You're her only heir."

"How do you know that?"

"Amanda, really? You're smarter than that."

She narrowed her eyes and looked at him oddly. "You murdered her, didn't you?"

UNKNOWN WORLD

"See? You're not that dumb after all. If only your aunt had signed the papers like I asked her to, we wouldn't be in this situation, and your boyfriend would be able to live to a ripe old age."

"Go to Hell!"

"Already been there." Zack shoved her back inside and thrust a legal looking document at her. "Sign this."

"No."

"Sign it," Zack ordered.

Amanda said nothing.

"If you sign it, I'll let you go. And to show you I'm a nice guy, I'll even let your boyfriend live."

Amanda was skeptical that Zack would keep his word, but she did know if she didn't sign the papers, he'd follow up on his threats. "What is this?" she asked.

"Bill of sale. You're selling me the five hundred acres for one hundred dollars."

"Why do you want it? The land is worthless."

"Maybe now it is, but not in the future. When the grid boots back up again, things will get back to normal and I'll be sitting pretty on five hundred prime acres. Austin is expanding and the land is right smack in the path of beautiful urban sprawl. I'm going to be a rich man some day."

"You can have it. Give me a pen."

Zack handed Amanda a pen.

"Cut the ties first."

"No. Sign it now."

Reluctantly, Amanda scribbled her name on the papers then shoved them back at Zack. He reached into his pockets and took out a hundred dollar bill.

"I don't want your money," she said. "Cut me loose. I did what you said."

"Not so fast. I still have some target practicing to do."

Catapulting off the chair, Amanda tried to kick him.

Zack pivoted out of the way then wrestled her back to the chair. He took a length of rope and tied her to the chair. "You used to be street smart. What happened?"

"Go to the devil!"

* * *

Upon seeing the 29-inch barrel of the Barrett M107 lining up on him, Uncle Billy leapt over the wall of the fountain and dove into the water. He felt the impact and the vibration of the .50 BMG round hitting the statue before the sound from the shot arrived. His only hope was to not be where Durant was aiming. Things were getting dicey and he wondered when Luke was going to get started.

Uncle Billy's question was answered momentarily. Luke had been sitting patiently on the roof of Dobie center, and when he saw his chance his .338 Lapua barked and blew a hole in the safety grate of the Tower.

Zack was momentarily startled at the shot until he understood what was happening. The man in the fountain was not Chandler. Whoever was in the Ghillie suit was meant to be a distraction. Zack adjusted his aim to the roof of the Dobie building. Having sighted and fired on this building before, he began laying down accurate fire on the rooftop.

Luke hit the ground immediately. Some of the incoming fire came too close for comfort. There was a gap in firing, presumably the M107's empty ten-round magazine was being replaced with a full one.

Uncle Billy recognized the deadliness of the M107 had been directed elsewhere. Seeing his chance, he rose out of the water, took upward aim through the side of the sculpture, and fired at the Tower. The OBR's 7.62 rounds popped the limestone walls, and chunks flew off, yet the target had not been hit.

Guards armed with military weapons, presumably acquired through looting, emptied into the courtyard. Most of these men entered the main tower building while the others headed toward Uncle Billy.

John engaged the guards using Uncle Billy's old Colt AR-15 Sporter, which was just as effective today as it was in the 1960s when it was new. John took aim and fired, forcing the guards headed toward Uncle Billy to take cover.

Moments earlier, Tatiana had recovered her weapons from John. She preferred an old Savage 99 take-down lever action carbine she had received for her birthday. Savage owners rarely sold their guns, so she was thrilled to find a used one in the gun shop with an original Ted Williams scope. The six shot .300 Savage felt lively in her hands, and she liked the brass cartridge counter which let her know how much ammo she had left.

Tatiana's backups were the MP-5 she had taken off the guard and a 12 gauge Stoeger double barrel, cut off at the end of the forend.

She had taken position to flank the guards now seeking cover from John. Her sessions with her grandmother's Mosin Nagant were paying off. The fine crosshairs of the Ted Williams scope made accurate hits easy. She kept the guards pinned down at first, then began taking headshots when their fire came close to her.

Now desperate, the last two guards made a banzai charge toward Tatiana while she reloaded. Their facial expressions turned to terror as they came close enough to see the business end of the Stoeger. Each guard took a blast of buckshot to the chest that ended his life.

Zack decided to take out the closest threat first. Squinting through the sights of the M107, he estimated where the man in the Ghillie suit was and started shooting through the statue. Chunks of bronze were blown off, the impacts offering a musical tone.

Luke swung up and knew the next shot was critical. He changed his target to the weapon first, hoping that he would still get a chance at Zack. Controlling his breath through the trigger squeeze, he sent the 250 grain missile toward the rifle. His shot was rewarded when the M107 twisted abruptly on its pintle mount.

Zack grunted when the large rifle jerked back, bruising his shoulder. He fell to the floor. The M107 had receiver metal bent inward behind the bolt carrier, making the rifle useless. Zack looked up to see a frightened Amanda pressed against the whiteness of the south wall, a wall that already contained several elliptical bullet holes from the 1966 shooting. Determined to make sure no one would have Amanda if he could not have her, he reached for his pistol.

Amanda screamed.

The metal door to the observation deck flung open and hit the side of the wall with a loud thud.

Chandler burst into the room and dove to the floor.

Amanda screamed again.

Zack swiveled his gun from Amanda to Chandler, and in the split second of indecision, Chandler sighted his Glock on Zack's head and pulled the trigger.

The first round grazed Zack's head, stunning him, and he

stumbled backward to the wall.

Zack brought his gun up and fired a wild shot.

Chandler fired again, aiming for the chest.

Zack's body took the full brunt of the shot.

Chandler fired again this time aiming for the head. He shot until the slide locked back.

Amanda sat wild-eyed and breathing hard. Seeing Zack's head obliterated was a sight she wouldn't forget.

Zack was no longer identifiable.

Chandler rushed to Amanda. "Are you alright? Are you hurt?"

"I think I'm okay," she said weakly. "Cut the ties off me, please. I have some papers to tear up."

* * *

Before Chandler had time to ask Amanda anything else, or to make an escape, the cavalry arrived to save Zack. They found a thick chain securing the metal screen door shut. When they tried to shoot off the lock, Chandler emptied a thirty round MP-5 magazine across the door at chest level. Three men fell, leaving at least twenty in the rear.

It was time to get nasty.

Chandler grabbed Zack's mattress and emptied several liquor bottles onto it. A blast from another MP-5 peppered the door.

Amanda hit the floor.

Chandler heaved the mattress against the door. He struck a match to a wad of paper then tossed it to the mattress, igniting it.

The outer cover burned quickly without much smoke. Once the center caught, the smoke turned dark gray and filled the observation deck.

The air became thick with soot.

Amanda coughed.

"Let's get outside!" Chandler yelled.

Chandler's training always required a backup plan. The blockage of the stairway now required the use of the backup plan, although the actual use of the plan was far from desirable.

Chandler looked straight into Amanda's eyes. "We don't have much time. I need you to trust me. Can you do that?" She nodded.

Chandler unzipped the main compartment of the backpack to

reveal a large coil of rope, rappel equipment, and a pair of gloves. "I've got three hundred feet of rope. It should be enough."

Beads of sweat broke out on Chandler's forehead.

"You're sweating," Amanda said. "I've never seen you sweat. What do you plan to do with the rope?"

Chandler only drew his hand across his forehead. He was a bit more than worried since the Travis Dam was the tallest structure he had rappelled off in the past, and that stunt almost put him in jail. His dad's 11mm 300 feet of rope was old, heavy, and considered substandard by today's climbers. Still, this plan had hastily been put together in a matter of hours and he was used to doing impossible things without all the necessary equipment.

Amanda did not look happy. "We're going to rappel? From *here*?" Her hands started to shake. "I can't. I...I won't."

Chandler took her by the arm. "You trust me, right?"

"Yes."

"Then don't worry. I'm going to do all the work. You just have to sit back and enjoy the ride." Chandler managed his best calming smile, but it was less than effective.

Working quickly, he strapped Amanda into a rescue harness then assembled his own webbed harness. He had his stainless steel figure eight for this job.

"Amanda, stand behind the corner there and cover your ears." Chandler took Zack's M-16 and blasted the welds on the wrought iron safety cage. Pieces of sizzling metal popped back at him, causing him to shake his arms to keep from getting burned by the random metal fragments.

While he emptied several M-16 magazines, Amanda took a Glock and holstered it along with the spare magazines. Several of the welds glowed red-orange as they started to cool from the friction of the bullets. Chandler bent back a few bars, creating enough space for them to fit through. He inserted a fresh magazine into the M-16 and handed it to Amanda.

"I'm going to walk us down slowly. There is no way you can fall, so don't think about that. I need you to watch the situation down below us and shoot anyone that tries to shoot us. I'll be too busy to help you, so you'll have to handle the bad guys yourself. Uncle Billy, Tatiana, and John are down there trying to keep them occupied. Can you do that?"

"I think so."

"Good," Chandler said. He took extra magazines and stuffed them in Amanda's pockets. He put the M-16's tactical sling over her shoulder and around her back. Even if she lost her grip on the rifle, the tactical sling would keep it close to her body rather than letting it fall.

Chandler clipped her back to his back.

The smoke from the mattress fire was starting to clear and had burned through the flammable material.

Time was short.

"Close your eyes for a moment," Chandler barked. He clipped his D-rings into the figure eight and lifted them onto the balcony. "Here we go."

There was a small jerk and the two of them popped three feet below the balcony edge. They were committed now. Amanda had not liked Chandler's tone when he barked the order, so she defied him and kept her eyes open. After watching her feet dangle over a three hundred foot drop, she wished she had kept her eyes closed.

"How are you doing? Is anyone down below?" Chandler asked.

"Everything's fine," Amanda blurted, fighting to keep her anxiety at a manageable level.

"We're going to bounce a few times. Pretend we're on a rollercoaster."

"I don't like rollercoasters," Amanda said. "And I don't—"

Chandler jumped three feet away from the building and the two dropped about ten feet. The couple repeated this bouncing procedure multiple times in rapid succession. They were making real progress toward the ground, but Chandler was worried.

Billowing smoke rushed out of the observation deck and filled the sky, clearing immediately. This meant the doors of the observation deck were now open.

They had seconds before the rope was discovered.

Amanda spotted two men below them. They were facing outward toward Uncle Billy's position, and then one saw a shadow and looked up. Amanda answered with a long burst, putting both of them on the ground.

"We need to move fast. Hold on!" Chandler's warning was followed by a sharp and long drop. He was worried that the freefall might be too long for the rope, then he saw heads peering through the opening in the safety grate. One last desperate belay on the figure eight caused both of them to feel like they were riding a whip.

Thankfully the rope held.

Chandler lightened his grip until they were safely on the ground.

Puffs of concrete erupted all around them. Chandler grabbed Amanda's hand and pulled her off to the side of the Tower.

* * *

John, Tatiana, and Uncle Billy breathed a sigh of relief. John and Tatiana stood up and began walking toward the fountain where Billy was waiting. The rescue was almost complete.

A loud voice broke the moment of silence. "Drop your weapons now!" Kurt Durant ordered. He was backed by nine thugs, all armed with fully automatic M-4 carbines. They had been hiding south of Inner Campus Drive, waiting for the rescuers to commit and show themselves.

Uncle Billy had to jump back into the fountain to avoid being completely exposed. John and Tatiana's weapons were outclassed. Chandler and Amanda each had three magazines left. The outlook did not look good, but surrender was not an option. If they were to die, they would not go alone.

"No, you drop *your* weapons!" Uncle Billy shouted back defiantly.

His order was met by hundreds of 5.56mm bullets. Chunks of stone broke away from the fountain.

Kurt's men had hit the dirt, making smaller targets of themselves.

John and Tatiana dropped to the ground, but had their field of view blocked by the back of the fountain, requiring them to move to a better position.

"Switch!" Chandler yelled. Amanda passed the M-16 to him and she covered him with the MP-5, knowing he needed to handle the tricky shots.

Chandler placed single shots through the gaps in the fountain and wounded a few of Kurt's men, keeping them pinned down until his parents could relieve Uncle Billy. Then he would move.

No fire came from Uncle Billy's position.

A wall of lead exploded toward Kurt's position. His men were taking fire from behind. Kurt wheeled around in time to take a slug to the stomach. He stumbled back and clutched the mortal wound to his mid-section. He fell to the ground and writhed for a few seconds, stiffened, then was still.

The relentless fire continued until the M-4s spoke no more.

Chandler recognized the sound of the guns used by his new allies. He jogged toward the fountain and joined his parents. They were relieved when Uncle Billy popped his head above the lip of the fountain.

"Thank you, Sassy boys!" Chandler yelled.

Six men and two women appeared, dressed in clothes better suited for a western. Some had Winchester rifles, others had a Colt Peacemaker or clone. Two had a six shooter in each hand.

Chandler glanced back to the main building to see the workers had picked up guns and were now taking Zack's men from the Tower into custody. It looked like UT's future would be in good hands.

* * *

"Chandler, you owe us about five pounds of lead," Ralph, the patriarch of the Sassy boys, chortled.

"I'll get busy on the press. Forty-five Long Colt?" Luke asked, having finally arrived at street level.

"Don't forget .357 Magnums for my Marlin!" Ralph's wife demanded, shaking the rifle in one hand.

During the celebratory back-slapping and high-fiving, nobody noticed the man lying on his back move.

Kurt Durant opened his eyes and looked around. A few steps in front of him was Amanda. She was the one who caused all this. Damn her. His gut felt like it was twisted and on fire, and if he was gut-shot he was a dead man and he knew it. He planned to take someone with him and let the others watch.

He drew his 1911 and forced himself upright. Unnoticed, he stumbled over to Amanda and clasped a bloody arm around her throat, shoving his 1911 against her temple.

Amanda screamed.

Chandler whipped around. "Don't hurt her!"

Amanda's eyes pleaded with Chandler to do something.

"Shut up." Kurt shoved the 1911 harder into Amanda's temple, forcing her head to the side.

Chandler took a menacing step forward.

"Stay back!" Kurt ordered. "I swear I'll kill her."

"Just let her go and we'll take you to the hospital. You're wounded and you'll bleed out if you don't get help."

Kurt snorted. "Like I believe that."

"Kurt, please," Amanda begged. "Let me go. It's over."

"Shut up! You ruined everything. If only I had gotten you at your grandpa's place, none of this—"

"What?" Amanda asked. Then a moment of clarity came to her. "That was *you* shooting at us? *You* killed my grandpa?"

"As per Zack's instructions," Kurt said triumphantly, dragging Amanda further back.

Chandler mirrored the steps.

By now Kurt's adrenaline rush waned and whatever superhuman strength he thought he had started to dwindle.

Chandler noticed him wobble, and Amanda felt his grip on her throat loosen. She kept her eyes on Chandler and when he nodded ever so slightly, she took that as a sign to do something. She thrust her hand palm side up to the side of her face and knocked the 1911 away from her temple.

Kurt's arm flung away and he discharged the 1911.

Amanda ducked and ran to Chandler. Before he could draw his weapon, Ralph sent Kurt a .45 semi-wadcutter straight to the heart. Kurt fell back, discharging his .45 ACP into the air. He was dead before he hit the ground.

Ralph went to Kurt and tapped him on the arm, looking for movement. Satisfied the guy was dead and all threats had been neutralized, he turned to Chandler. "Now where were we before we were so rudely interrupted? Ah yes, how about we take the M-4s?"

"How about we split it all down the middle? We were here a little longer than you," Chandler said.

Ralph returned a grin. "Sounds like a plan."

Chandler put his arms around Amanda. "We made it, unharmed, and it looks like none of us took a bullet."

Uncle Billy chimed in. "Maybe not all of us," he said, waddling toward the group while holding his backside.

"Where'd ya get shot?" Chandler asked.

"Where the sun don't shine."

"Leave it to Uncle Billy to get it in the butt," Luke complained sarcastically.

"And a cute butt it is." Amanda laughed. Looking up at Chandler she said, "Must run in the family."

"I don't know about you, but I've had enough fun to last me a while," Chandler said.

"You call this fun?" Amanda asked. "I think I need to teach you a thing or two."

"Still sassy after all this time."

"And don't ever expect that to change."

"I wouldn't want to change one thing about you," Chandler said. "Come on, everybody, let's head home."

THE END

THE LAKE

A BONUS SCENE

Five years before the EMP

Under the cover of darkness, a man with inked arms and a snake tattoo on his neck crawled down the embankment leading to the dark, languid waters of Lake Travis. Created by the impounding of the Colorado River by constructing Mansfield Dam circa 1940, Lake Travis at its deepest was two hundred and ten feet, and had two hundred and seventy miles of shoreline—a perfect spot for what he needed to dispose of.

He had driven along the winding RR 620, then parked his car in a remote section of a park located near the lake on the outskirts of Austin. He cut the engine and the lights, and rolled down the window. The summer heat immediately dispatched the air-conditioning he had been enjoying on the thirty minute drive from his dilapidated house to the park.

It was quiet and dark at the late hour.

Without any streetlamps or ambient light from shopping centers or houses, it took a few seconds for his eyes to adjust to the inky blackness. The sliver of a moon sat low in the sky; twinkling stars glittered. He let his eyes roam over the parking lot and the thick bramble of cedars and scrub oaks dotting the limestone hillside, prevalent in the Hill Country of Texas.

A lone camper was the only other sign of civilization.

The primitive spot would work well.

If he had been inclined to, and if the baggie in the glove compartment wasn't beckoning to him, and if it had been light, he would have ventured onto the hillside looking for fossils of the Cretaceous or Mesozoic Era.

It was difficult to fathom the central part of Texas being a primitive inland sea some 140 million years ago, (give or take a few million years) making it the former home to prehistoric creatures and fish. After the soft tissues of mollusk-like marine animals decayed, sediments filled the internal cavity and over eons of time, hardened fossil trophies remained.

But fossil hunting would have to wait. He reached into the glove compartment, grabbed a pre-rolled joint, and struck a match to it. Taking a deep drag, he expanded his lungs, held his breath, then exhaled.

Several drags later a warm fog washed over him.

Sitting there alone in his car, the man with the long stringy hair and tat-covered arms briefly thought about the contents in the back seat.

Always a loner, the man had been a perfect match for the once small reptile which had been smuggled into the states at a great cost. For years the man had toiled to create an environment which mimicked the natural habitat from which the python had been liberated. One room of his old house had infrared lights, a large kiddie pool with a filter system that put the best pools to shame, jungle worthy foliage, and a boulder for the reptile to sun on.

The years passed, and the cute twenty-four inch reptile had grown into an unmanageable, five foot strong coil of muscle and teeth. The last straw was when the man came home from work to find his cat missing and a large bulge in the snake's midsection.

Reggie the snake was no longer welcome.

Without any further hesitation or thought, he finished the joint, pinched the end, and put the remainder in his pocket for later use. He retrieved a burlap sack from the back seat, shut the door as softly as he could, and began the arduous task of dragging the heavy sack across the pavement.

Salty sweat beaded his forehead and trickled down the sides of his face and into his eyes, stinging them. He drew a hand across his forehead, wiping it away.

Stooped over and breathing hard, he struggled to drag the burlap-enclosed python across the bumpy terrain, picking his way around the Christmas-tree shaped cedars and thorny cactus. The python hissed at the thrashing from the hard limestone rocks and thorny cactus.

The air was hot and still, and the man sneezed violently from the cedar pollen blanketing the ground in a yellow haze.

At last he came to the hillside, and with gravity as his friend, the steep slope toward Lake Travis wasn't quite as daunting to navigate. To keep his balance, he had to sit on his rear and scoot down the dark hillside, feet first.

Coming to a limestone ledge, he heaved the burlap sack in front of him.

A wave of nostalgia overcame him, but he shook it off once he remembered the bulge in the snake's belly. His cat didn't deserve to die like that.

He flicked open a knife and cut the strings, loosening them until the sack was open. He cursed at not bringing a flashlight and was surprised at how dark the hillside was. Lights across the expansive lake twinkled, and mumbled voices and laughter drifted along the surface of the dark water.

Satisfied he was alone, he bent at the waist and reached into the sack—

The python rocketed out of the sack, opened its mouth and sunk its teeth into his shoulder.

The man dropped the knife and it clattered on the limestone rock. Dazed at the strike and the needling pain, he stumbled backwards off the limestone cliff and into the hard limbs of a cedar tree.

The snake held steadfast, dangling from his shoulder. Its tail whipping the ground, the snake instinctively curled its body around the man's waist and one of his legs, pinning an arm.

Tighter the snake coiled, squeezing.

The man screamed into the black void. He balled his fist and pummeled the snake in the head.

The snake dug its fangs deeper into the man's shoulder.

He screamed in pain.

Off balance from the massive reptile hanging from his shoulder, the man fell to the dark soil peppered with cedar berries and saw-toothed leaves embedded in and around chunky limestone rocks.

He struggled and thrashed, rolling around on the sloping hill, perilously close to the edge of the limestone cliff, only to hit his head on a larger rock. His free hand swept the ground, searching in vain for a rock, a stick, or anything to loosen the snake's grip on him.

Breathing became difficult and he took several shallow breaths. With tremendous effort he managed to stand up, which only caused blood to rush to his head. He wobbled on unsteady legs. His eyes rolled up and he fell listlessly upon the sloping cliff. His body tumbled along the limestone, washed smooth by eons of rain and erosion.

The man and snake fell thirty feet through the air, and hit the cold, dark waters of the deep lake.

The jolt of falling the equivalent distance from a three-story building and hitting water shocked the man back to reality and he instinctively held his breath.

He struggled to loosen the snake, his arms thrashing the water.

He was vaguely aware of sinking deeper in the water. He kicked his legs, dropping deeper still until the pressure popped his ears.

He desperately needed to breathe, his body screamed for oxygen, and for seconds that seemed like hours the man fought the urge to inhale. His body's need for oxygen overrode all other senses and the man inhaled a lungful of water.

His body convulsed and for a brief moment of clarity he realized he was drowning.

After that, there was nothing, no consciousness, no witnesses to the life or death fight, only blackness and the ripple of water at the surface as the dark lake swallowed him.

The python uncoiled from the lifeless man. It felt no emotion or remorse, or joy at being the victor, only a reptilian need to live.

An expert swimmer, the python glided to the surface of the lake where its nostrils and eyes breached the surface. Flicking its tongue, it took in its surroundings, tasting the air and forming an image of the lake and land using an organ to sense infrared thermal radiation.

The hazy waters bobbed and ebbed, and the python let its body move with the waves instead of fighting them. Soon it came to an inlet of the lake where the grassy land sloped gently, meeting the water.

The python's sensory system detected movement on the shore and its primitive brain expertly formed a thermal image of the animal foraging for food. The ten pound animal about the size of a raccoon remained clueless that a predator lurked in the water.

The snake slithered closer.

Remaining perfectly still, the python floated, keeping to the rhythm of the waves lapping the shore, biding its time as the hapless animal came closer to the water's edge.

The water erupted and in the second it took the animal to react, the python struck with lightning fast speed, sinking its fangs into the neck of the animal. The animal, now in the deep throes of fight or flight, let out a surprised squeak. Its heart raced, and it jerked and thrashed to free itself from the unknown predator, but the snake only sank its fangs deeper into the warm flesh. It squeezed harder, more, until the animal was completely encased in the coils of the python. No longer able to breathe, the animal went limp and lost consciousness.

Death came quickly.

The python began the difficult task of positioning the animal headfirst for consumption. Like something out of a horror movie, the python contracted its strong muscles to swallow the animal inch by inch, and when the tail disappeared down the python's throat, the reptile relaxed.

Hours later and with a bulging midsection, the python searched for a cove where it could hide, away from civilization, away from the species which had imprisoned it.

The scenario played out repeatedly over the years, the python snatching unsuspecting wild animals or pets. It rested, hid, and digested its meal until the urge to hunt struck again. It hibernated during the cold winters and when the waters warmed, it emerged, searching, always on the hunt.

Five years from when the man met his own death in the dark waters of the deep lake, the python had grown into an impressive and massive reptile, one which the wild animals of the lake shores had come to fear and respect. It cruised the shoreline and the coves, and at times ventured into the tributary of the lake—the Colorado River, which was also the southern boundary of the Big View Ranch.

* * *

During the months after the shootout at the Tower, Chandler convinced Amanda to stay at the family compound, and the EMP survivors gradually became accustomed to the new normality of life without modern conveniences.

Each family member had their own task to complete during the day. As matriarch of the house, Tatiana managed the food supply, which she rationed with an iron hand.

Luke and Chandler were in charge of hunting and firearms training, so each family member became familiar with the different types of pistols and rifles.

John and Uncle Billy managed security for the house and for the neighborhood.

Amanda used her gardening abilities to plant seasonal vegetables, and with Tatiana's help they canned the vegetables the family was unable to consume.

Neighbors came together and helped each other out by trading goods or services, and for those that had a working truck or car, forays into the city had become a dangerous necessity. More and more desperate survivors turned to the river and lake as a source of food and water. Sporadic gunshots echoed off the hills, interrupting the silence prevalent in the new world.

On this particular night, the Chandler family was outside on the patio, playing a game of dominos. This time during the evening was the time the family rested and came together to talk about the day and what needed to be accomplished in the coming days.

The bitter cold had been replaced by a temperate spring. The pecan trees were heavy with tender foliage, grass had greened, and the long winter had finally relinquished its hold on the land.

Tatiana had made lemonade using lemons from the tree she had once cursed as producing too much fruit.

Nipper had jumped into Amanda's lap, pillowed into it, and put his head on his paws. She stroked him along his back and scratched him behind his ears.

"Hun," John said, "I think it's time we turned in."

Tatiana yawned. "I'm getting sleepy too. Let's head on up to bed. See everybody in the morning."

"Good night," Amanda said.

Uncle Billy stretched and agreed with his brother it was time to turn in.

The younger generation—Amanda, Chandler, and Luke—stayed and talked a while.

"I wonder how Kate is doing?" Luke said.

"Mom's been worried about her," Chandler said. "When she's in the kitchen she stares out the kitchen window. I know she's looking for Kate."

"Mom and Dad have been talking about making a trip to San Antonio to try to find her," Luke said. "They think she's probably still at the Minor Hotel."

"If she's still there, it's probably by choice," Chandler said.

"Yeah, I pity whoever she's with." Luke laughed at the thought. "She can be as tough as a wildcat."

Chandler glanced at Amanda, who flicked her eyes to Luke. Her expression was one of *It's time for him to leave.* Chandler shifted positions on the bench. "Luke, it *is* getting late. Aren't you tired?"

"Oh, bad timing again?"

"You could say that."

"Okay, I get the message. I'll leave you two lovebirds alone."

"When you go in, be sure to put away the .357 you were cleaning on the dining room table. And bring me my Glock you cleaned," Chandler said.

"I'm not your gopher," Luke grumbled. "I already put it on your bed. Some thanks I get. You get to clean the guns next time."

"Yeah, yeah," Chandler said waving him off. "Better not let Mom catch you messing up her house again. You know how she gets."

Luke harrumphed. He walked back into the house, knowing there was no way he was going to do any more work tonight, and if big brother wanted his gun, he'd have to get it himself. Luke was tired and wanted to go to bed. He'd put the .357 and cleaning supplies away first thing in the morning.

Amanda and Chandler sat side by side at the picnic table. A breeze rustled the leaves of the pecan trees, and somewhere in the distance a cricket chirped. Stars twinkled in the night sky. They sat in silence, enjoying each other's company.

"It's so dark," Amanda said. "I wish we had more light."

"Our battery supply is getting low, and Dad has been bugging me about not using our flashlights unless we really need them. He definitely adheres to the 'Work while there's light' saying'."

"I remember my grandpa saying that," Amanda said. "I still miss him."

"I know you do. He was a great man. I wish I could have known him." Chandler paused. "Amanda, I'm glad you stayed."

"Me too." She held out her hand, inviting him to take it. He threaded his strong, warm fingers through hers then brought her hand to his lips. He kissed her fingers starting at the pinky, then to her ring finger until he kissed each one.

"That tickles." Amanda giggled.

"Maybe one of these days I can tickle you all over."

Amanda smiled. "Promises, promises."

Nipper, who had been resting peacefully on Amanda's lap, sat up. His ears were cocked and he was looking intently toward the river. He growled low in his throat then pushed off with his hind legs, leapt through the air, and bolted to the direction of the river's edge.

"Nipper! Stop!" Amanda yelled. Rising from the bench, she went to the edge of the yard and cupped her hands around her mouth. "Come back!" she hollered.

"Don't worry. He'll be back," Chandler said.

"He can be such a bad dog," Amanda said in exasperation. Although it was too dark to see Nipper, she could hear him scurrying and darting in and among the leaves and brush. He barked louder, strong warning barks.

Chandler went to where Amanda was standing and wrapped his arms around her waist. Moonlight reflected off the quiet river, casting a glow onto her face.

"Don't worry about him. He's okay." Chandler leaned over and took her face in his hands and kissed her fully on the lips, a strong kiss filled with passion and want—the way a man should kiss a woman. He kissed her hungrily, greedily, without hesitation. Amanda responded and slid her hands to the small of his back.

The heady interlude only lasted a moment when Nipper squealed a high-pitched vociferous bark.

Amanda leaned away from Chandler. "Something must be wrong. He's never made that noise before. I'll be right back."

"Oh, no you don't," Chandler protested. "The last time you went looking for Nipper you got kidnapped and all hell broke loose. Stay here, and don't move. I want to pick up where we left off."

Chandler flicked on his flashlight and carefully picked his way toward the river, dodging rocks and brush. Nipper kept barking. The flashlight beam jerkily bounced from place to place as Chandler searched for Nipper. A flash of white darting at the base of a pecan tree caught his eye and Chandler trotted in that direction.

Nipper sat under a tree, he was panting and long strings of drool dripped from his mouth.

"What's wrong, boy? What'd ya find?"

Nipper curled sideways and glanced back at Chandler. He panted heavily and his ruff was raised. His body posture was odd.

Chandler flicked the flashlight at the tree then to the surrounding thick brush. "There's nothing there, boy," he said. He bent down to pet Nipper and to calm him. "There's nothing—"

The force of the impact knocked Chandler to the ground and caused him to lose his breath. It felt as if a hundred pound bag of flour had wacked him on the back, and he gasped to catch his breath. The flashlight had tumbled to the ground and rolled away, the beam disappearing into the darkness.

Nipper snarled and snapped, darting back and forth.

Chandler was face down on the ground and it took him a long second to regain his wits. He immediately reached for his Glock, but his arms wouldn't move. Then he remembered Luke had put it on his bed. He opened his eyes to the horror that his arms were pinned by a massive python. Chandler threw his weight to the side, trying to loosen the death grip the large reptile had on him. He was vaguely aware he was perilously close to the river and a brief thought crossed his mind the reptile was trying to smother him then roll him into the river. He dug the heels of his boots into the dirt to stop the snake's progress.

Seconds of a life and death struggle passed between the two species—one a sentient being, the other a cold blooded reptile, where another life meant nothing, other than to satiate the animalistic need to eat.

The reptile coiled tighter around its prey.

Chandler's breathing became labored and he gasped shallow quick breaths.

Nipper continued barking and darting, biting at the snake.

"Somebody help me!" Chandler squeaked.

The reptile had completely coiled around Chandler's chest and neck, cutting off his ability to expand his lungs.

Chandler blinked, and with one remaining breath he muttered, "Help." The plea was weak and unbecoming to a voice that normally boomed. Air leaked out of his lungs and he tried to breathe, but his lungs were paralyzed. Stars appeared in his vision and consciousness waned. The branches of the tree above him swayed, reaching to him as if beckoning him skyward to something beyond, something unknown and out of his grasp. If only he could grab a limb to pull himself up; if only he had the strength to fight, but he was too weary, too tired.

His eyelids fluttered and he finally closed his eyes and gave in to the overwhelming need to sleep. His last thought was of Amanda and the regret he had about being unable to tell her how he felt about her. A man who was known for his bravery on the battlefield, one who could expertly dispatch an enemy without so much as a blink of an eye, couldn't tell the women he loved how he felt.

That was the regret of his life.

* * *

Amanda remained at the edge of the yard as Chandler had instructed her. She had listened to Nipper's incessant barking and Chandler's pleading and increasingly annoyed calls to the dog. When they came back, she'd lock Nipper in the laundry room for the entire night. He had caused enough trouble. What a bad dog he was.

After a minute had passed, it became obvious Chandler had stopped calling for the dog. The flashlight's stationary beam worried her since she had seen the methodical search pattern Chandler had used earlier to try to locate Nipper. There was something odd going on. Nipper continued barking in a manner Amanda had never heard before. The odd barking and yelps sounded so…so painful, like he was trying to communicate something.

That was it.

Something *must* be wrong.

"Chandler!" Amanda yelled. "Chandler! What's going on?"

She waited, listening.

"Can you hear me?" Her pleas were met by Chandler's silence and Nipper's increasingly raucous barks.

Her first instinct was to go to him, but without a weapon she could succumb to whatever Chandler and Nipper had found. She dashed into the house and searched for a weapon. There, on the dining room table was the .357 magnum Luke had been cleaning after dinner. She picked it up and quickly determined it was loaded, bolted out of the house, across the patio, and half tumbled, half slid down the embankment leading to the river.

She came upon a scene so disturbing she froze. A python had coiled around Chandler, who was as still and white as a corpse. The resigned expression on his face shocked her.

Nipper kept barking.

"God help me," Amanda whispered.

She retrieved the flashlight, shined it on the massive reptile, and searched for its head. Beady eyes glowed red in the flashlight beam. It was now or never. She aimed and fired. The single well-placed shot obliterated the head of the python.

Nipper flinched when scales and skin hit him on the face. Step by cautious step he went to the snake and sniffed, curious about the lifeless reptile. It smelled of the lake and of the animals it had eaten. He flicked his tongue and tasted the bloody body. He found it neither repulsive nor revolting, only something to be filed away in his brain for future use.

Working quickly Amanda struggled to uncoil the snake's muscles that had yet to retract. Mustering strength she didn't know she had, she loosened the hold the reptile had on Chandler's head and chest. She heaved him onto his stomach and uncoiled the snake at the same time, repeating the action until Chandler was free.

Nipper sat to the side, panting.

Amanda put her index and middle finger to Chandler's neck. There was no pulse.

"Don't die on me! You hear me Christopher Chandler!"

She crisscrossed her hands and placed them on his chest. Stiff-arming, she used all her upper body strength and compressed his chest thirty times in quick succession. She moved to his head, tilted it back to clear his airway. She pinched his nose shut, inhaled as deeply as she could, sealed her lips around his, and blew into his mouth.

She looked for his chest rising. It did, so she gave him another rescue breath, and waited for him to breathe normally.

When he did not breathe on his own, she compressed his chest thirty more times and breathed into his mouth.

She waited. Nothing happened.

She cycled CPR another time.

Minutes passed as she continued cycling. Her muscles burned from the strain.

Sweat dripped off of her forehead.

Nipper sat to the side, watching, confused.

She did CPR one last cycle and waited for him to breathe normally.

She had failed. She sat back and sobbed openly. The tears came rushing out, blurring her vision.

Nipper padded to Chandler and cocked his head. He gingerly pawed and waited for a reaction. Perhaps a verbal reply or a hand gesture acknowledging his presence.

He pawed again, then barked at the man and waited for him to wake.

The man was not dead, yet he was not alive, and curiosity overcame Nipper. He licked Chandler on the cheek, warm, thoughtful licks tasting the man he had come to respect, one he had come to know as Amanda's partner. Their bond was unmistakable and Nipper had seen it in the way he spoke to her, the way he looked at her.

Nipper licked more, tasting the man's aura, his very being, the life that made him the strong and confident man he was. Nipper stepped away, knowing his efforts had failed. His ears flopped down and a feeble expression captured him. The struggle between man and reptile had been brutal and Nipper had been powerless to help.

Turning away from Chandler, Nipper sensed Amanda's emotional turmoil. She had collapsed on the ground and curled into a fetal position, sobbing. Nipper did as he had done many times before and leaned into her and put his head on her lap to comfort her. He nudged her hand with his wet nose until he elicited a response. Hesitantly, she rested her hand on his head, stroking him between his eyes then stroked him along the ruff of his back, taking comfort in her pet's loyalty and compassion.

* * *

Amanda looked like Chandler had always imagined. She was next to him in bed, her soft pale skin flush against his. Waves of her thick hair cascaded over her shoulders. They were under the sheets, and she playfully tickled him by running her finger over his chest.

Music played in the background, something tantalizing, capturing the moment, something he hadn't heard before. Then they were doing a tango or some other dance he was normally clumsy at. Yet his feet flew over the dance floor as if he was meant to dance, as if he had done the dance all his life. He held her tight against him and they moved in tandem, expertly, sensually.

She wore a slinky black dress made of exotic material and patterned with bright scarlet roses.

It was like they were in a vacuum, only the two of them. No one else mattered. Nothing else mattered. His hands explored her body and he brought her close to him and kissed her fully on the lips.

A dog barked close to his ear, interrupting the heady moment. After a while the barking abated and he went back to Amanda. They were back in bed, between the cool sheets. He went to move—

The damn barking starting again and the loudest gunshot he had ever heard made his eardrums ring.

He felt like he was suffocating. His head pounded and his eardrums rang.

Something pressed down hard on his chest. It was Amanda leaning over him. He felt lightheaded and had a strange sensation of his chest being compressed. What the hell was she doing with the hands he had dreamed of being wrapped around him? She had pinned him down and he couldn't move. So this was how she wanted to play? He never imagined she was like this, and if he was her playground, he'd ask if she wanted the bars or the merry-go-round.

In a flash they were back in bed and she laughed and said something he didn't understand.

Then something wet and warm licked his face and at first he thought it was Amanda until he got a whiff of dog breath. Damn dog. He tried to shoo away the dog, but his arms wouldn't move.

There she was again on top of him. He pulled her closer, her lips on his and she was unapologetically wanting him.

But his lips hurt, and his chest felt odd, burning for a breath.

He wanted to tell her to stop because he needed to breathe. She was heavier than he thought and suffocating him. Her lips had an airlock on his. He needed her to get off him.

He needed to breathe.

When he tried to speak, the words wouldn't form.

Finally, she moved off him, and the weight on his chest dissipated. There, that was better.

Chandler took a small breath, then another, until the effort became so natural it was unnoticed. The air had never felt so clean and new, and his lungs no longer burned. His hand went to his chest and he rubbed it. He had on a shirt and thought that was strange. He must have fallen asleep and had been dreaming about Amanda.

The struggle to open his eyes required a herculean effort, like he was drugged or something. Maybe he was just tired. Yes, that was it. He blinked his eyes open and the magnificent sky of twinkling stars of the Milky Way came into focus. For a few minutes he stared in wonder at the glorious sight.

Amanda was next to him, shivering. She was crying and had curled into a little ball. Maybe she was cold. He gently put his arm around her, pushing Nipper out of the way. She didn't even notice.

"Amanda," he said, "why are you crying?"

She catapulted up and stared at him with an odd mixture of relief and frustration. Her face was flushed and she swiped her hand beneath both eyes.

"Are you okay?" Chandler asked, propping himself up on his elbows.

"You're *alive*?"

"Huh? Of course I'm alive."

Amanda burst out crying.

"What's wrong? Why are you crying?"

"Don't you remember?" she managed to ask between sobs.

"Remember what?"

"That." Amanda pointed to the ground a few feet away.

Chandler's eyes tracked to where she was pointing. It was dark and he wasn't quite sure his eyes weren't playing tricks on him. He reached for his flashlight.

"What is that?" He shined the flashlight in the direction she pointed. "Is that a…" His words caught in his throat when he remembered. "The python. I remember now." He looked at Nipper then up at the tree then back to Amanda. "It must have been in the tree. I remember being knocked to the ground. It was so strong. I couldn't…I called out…nobody came."

"I came." Amanda knelt next to him. "Shhh." She touched his lips, quieting him. "You don't need to talk. It doesn't matter."

"Did you kill it?"

"With one shot from a Colt Python. Luke left it on the dining room table."

"Poetic justice, don't you think?" Chandler asked.

"Yes, and for once his messiness came in handy." Amanda laughed.

"I had this wild dream about you," Chandler said.

"Oh? What about?"

"You might be embarrassed if I told you."

"Tell me anyway."

"First there's something else I want to tell you. Something I've been meaning to say for a long time now." Chandler patted the ground. "Sit next to me."

Amanda sat down next to him, tucking her legs under herself.

Chandler flicked the flashlight and shined it in all directions.

"What are you looking for?"

"Luke. I want to make sure he's not around."

Amanda looked at him curiously.

"He has bad timing."

"That he does."

"Amanda…" Chandler sat up and took her hands in his. "I want you to know I luh—"

Luke came rushing over. Out of breath he asked. "What happened? I heard Nipper barking then a shot. And somebody crying." His eyes went to the dead python. "What the hell?"

Amanda and Chandler burst out laughing.

"What did I do?" Luke asked.

Amanda and Chandler only looked at him.

221

"Bad timing?"

"The worst," Chandler said. "Now get lost."

"Alright, alright. I'm leaving." Luke huffed. "Just trying to be a good brother."

"Take Nipper with you," Chandler said. "He's been enough trouble for one night."

After Luke left with Nipper, Chandler pulled Amanda to him. He leaned into her and pressed his mouth to her and whispered, "I love you."

She brushed the hair away from his forehead. "Say it again. I'm not sure I heard you the first time."

"I love you," he repeated.

"I love you too."

"Come on," Chandler said. "I know a secluded place near the river where the grass is soft and where a cypress tree hangs over a cove. We won't be disturbed."

"Oh," Amanda commented. "Sounds tantalizing."

"Speaking of tantalizing, I want to tell you about the dream I had about you."

"Was it dirty?" she asked playfully.

Rising, he grinned and invited her to stand. Taking her hand, he pulled her close to him. He leaned into her and whispered, "The dirtiest."

THE END

BEHIND THE SCENES
A NOTE FROM THE AUTHOR

Hi readers, this is Chris.

The inspiration for the EMP Survivor series came to me while traveling across the expansive Atchafalaya Basin Bridge on I-10 on our way to New Orleans. At the time, my youngest daughter was going to Tulane. I wondered what it would be like if a person was lost in the swamp and had to walk out. A simple road trip led to the creation of the series.

When I create characters, it sometimes takes me trying out several names until I finally decide on the right one.

Bad guy Cole Cassel's name (he's in Books 1 and 2) was a combination of two players on the Dallas Cowboys team from the 2015 roster. I have had a love/hate relationship with that team ever since I can remember. My parents were huge fans, so I grew up watching them play.

Regarding other character names, I toyed with several names for Dillon Stockdale and Holly Hudson. Their names changed during the writing of the story. Dillon Marshal didn't sound right (flip it and you'll understand) and neither did Holly Halliburton. It took me a while to find a name for Cassie, and I tried out several names until the name sounded right.

Since Amanda is twenty-one, I Googled popular baby names in 1995 when she would have been born. The name Amanda immediately struck me as the right name.

When I started writing about Chandler, the name popped into my head so I decided to use it. Then I thought: is that his last name or first name? I decided it was his last name, so I came up with an easy to remember first name…Chris. But it didn't sound right to call him Chris since I had been writing Chandler. So I decided to keep using his last name.

Regarding the UT Tower scene, I took a tour of the Tower to make sure the descriptions were right. It's actually quite humbling to stand there in the same place where the real tragedy unfolded in 1966. And yes, several bullet holes are still there.

The neighborhood on Big View where the Chandler family lives is an actual neighborhood on the Colorado River in west Austin, although the Big View Ranch and history is fictional. The Panther Hollow story is real and I stumbled across it while researching the area.

* * *

I have received emails asking me to write faster. I take that as a compliment and a challenge, because with a fulltime job, it's difficult to put a novel together during spare time. Yet, as empty nesters there is now time to do that.

When the words seem effortlessly put together, when you find yourself reading as fast as you can to see what happens next, then I've done my job. If only I could write as fast as y'all can read, everyone would be happy.

During 2016, I wrote and published Books 1 and 2 of the EMP Survivor series, and finished Book 3 that was published in early 2017. Three novels in one year is a lot. Believe me.

Many of you have written asking me how to write. Writing is a skill that can be learned, just like learning math or English, but it takes practice and dedication. The best thing to do is to join a local writers group and connect with writers. Go to a conference and listen to people who have experience.

Above all, you must write.

We all have a story to tell. Somewhere I read this: "*Someone out there needs your story.*" That is so true. It doesn't matter what your style is, or how good your vocabulary is, or how many other good writers there are. This is a quote by Henry Van Dyke I keep on my desk whenever I think my writing isn't as good as any other author: "*Use what talents you possess: the woods would be very silent if no birds sang there except those that sang best.*"

How true is that?

Several years ago I entered my first story in a local writing contest, thinking I had written the next best American novel.

I was wrong. Big time.

Try an F minus wrong, with emphasis on the minus.

When I received my grading sheet I was mad at first, then I read and re-read the judge's comments. They were right, the story was poor and so was the writing. I was determined to turn it around, so I worked really hard, learning how to write, learning about white space, dialogue tags, pacing, you name it, I tried to learn it. My next entry garnered an honorable mention.

It's also important to read and to study bestselling authors. How is the story started? How are characters introduced? What about length of paragraphs and sentences? What's the right balance between dialogue and narration? How is action written? (Short, tight sentences…that's how).

I've found it best to mix things up since too much of anything fatigues the readers, like long paragraphs or chapters that seem to never end. Have you ever opened your Kindle to be greeted by one whole screen of never-ending words? Groan. That's what I mean by fatigue.

White space is important because our eyes naturally gravitate to the empty spaces on the page.

Shorter is better in our fast paced life where information is available at the touch of a button. A four hundred page novel by an unknown author is too daunting a challenge for most people, including me. I'd rather buy two books that are two hundred pages each at $3.99 than one gigantic novel at $5.99.

Don't try to impress people with linguistic gymnastics, just tell the story. They won't be impressed, and you'll end up looking like a fool.

Our time is important, so as authors we must write the best first sentence possible. We have to give the reader a clue as to what the story is about, and to end the first scene in a way it alludes to what will happen in the story. Or a plot question needs to be introduced. If none of that is conveyed, readers will go on to another novel, and that's bad.

I pay attention to reviews because I learn a lot from my readers: what you liked, what you didn't like, and so for the next book I try to add more of what you want, and less of what you don't. For example, there are no F-bombs in this book since that is what you asked for. I listened.

So reviews are important.

Please take a moment to post a review.

Emails are important too. If I've made a mistake, let me know, especially a fact-based mistake like turning on a kerosene lantern. It's lit with a match, not turned on as I learned from one of my readers.

I try to write every day, sometimes it's only a couple of paragraphs, other times it's four or five pages. So after several months of writing, a novel takes shape.

Some authors outline their story. I don't. I have an idea then start writing, and the more I write, the more the story takes shape. I get to know the characters, their motivations, problems, anything that makes them who they are.

During the writing of *Unknown World*, I wrote an entire scene about Chandler coming home from his tour, borrowing his brother's truck, driving to East Texas where he walks in and finds his girlfriend and best friend in bed together.

It was a great scene, and I tried to find a place for it in the book, but it only disrupted the flow of the story because it was back story—it happened prior to the EMP. It was still an important scene because it allowed me to get to know Chandler better. He's not as transparent as other characters. He's reticent and private, and is devastated by the betrayal, turning the pain inward and it nearly destroyed him. If you want to read the scene, email me and I'll send you the scene.

So even though it killed me to cut 3,000 words, I had to do it. And I think the story is better. What transpired between him and his girlfriend, and how he got over it is conveyed through action and snippets of dialogue.

So, what's next?

I'm working on Book 4 which will take place in San Antonio where Kate Chandler works as a bartender at the historic "Minor" Hotel (modeled after the real Menger Hotel) not far from the Riverwalk. Take a minute and Google the Menger. It's fascinating.

The Alamo is located in the heart of San Antonio, right next to the Menger. So there's opportunity for plenty of action.

There is so much that can be done with the characters and the settings in Texas and Louisiana. I still want to write a story about

Garrett, a character introduced in Book 2. He's an interesting guy, someone that would become a natural leader, but I may instead wrap up the series in Book 5. We'll be heading back to East Texas to see how Holly, Dillon, Ryan, and Cassie are doing, plus the cause of the EMP will be revealed. A lot can change in a year, so stay tuned.

Readers, thank you for continuing this journey. And as several characters have said, remember the three F's: Faith, family, and firearms.

ABOUT THE AUTHOR

Chris Pike grew up in the woodlands of Central Texas and along the Texas Gulf Coast, fishing, hiking, camping, and dodging hurricanes and tropical storms. Chris has learned that the power of Mother Nature is daunting from sizzling temperatures or icy conditions; from drought to category five hurricanes. Living without electricity for two weeks in the sweltering heat after Hurricane Ike proved to be challenging. It paid to be prepared.

Currently living in Houston, Texas, Chris is married, has two grown daughters, one son-in-law, one dog, and three overweight, demanding cats.

Chris has held a Texas concealed carry permit since 1998, with the Glock being the current gun of choice. Chris is a graduate of the University of Texas and has a BBA in Marketing. By day Chris works as a database manager for a large international company, while by night an Indie author.

Got a question or a comment? Email Chris at Chris.Pike123@aol.com. Your email will be answered promptly and your address will never be shared with anyone. Or connect with me on Facebook at Author Chris Pike like hundreds of other readers have.

UNWANTED WORLD BOOK 4

Unwanted World will be a standalone book continuing the saga of the Chandler family. Stay tuned for the story of Kate Chandler and new character Niko Bell as they learn to live in this new world. They too will encounter dangerous people and situations. The book will be available in mid-July 2017.

BEFORE YOU GO...

One last thing. Thank you, thank you, thank you for downloading this book. Without the support of readers like yourself, Indie publishing would not be possible.

I've heard from a lot of my readers, and for those who have written to me, you know I always answer your emails. You have taught me a lot with your expertise in electronics, medicine, and basically how things work. Your encouragement has inspired me to keep writing. Thank you.

Another way to show your support of an Indie author is to write an honest review on Amazon. It helps other readers make a decision to download the book. A few words or one sentence is all it takes.

So please consider writing a review. I will be forever grateful.

Also, this book has been edited, proofed, and proofed again, but mistakes or typos are bound to happen. If you find a mistake, email me at Chris.Pike123@aol.com and it will be corrected. Or like hundreds of other reads have done, connect with me on Facebook at Author Chris Pike.

Lastly, a big shout out goes to the people who helped with questions, editing, formatting, audio, cover art, proofing, legal advice, encouragement, and everything else that goes into making a book: Alan, Michelle, Courtney, Cody, Felicia, Kody, Kevin, Hristo, Anne, Mary, Mikki, and Mick B.

For my readers who have written me, y'all are the best! You've encouraged me and have allowed me a glimpse into your life. I am truly honored. Thank you.

Until the next time, and as one of my readers wrote: Read, enjoy, learn, and save some more food.

All the best,
Chris

Made in the USA
Las Vegas, NV
04 June 2022

49783965R00134